The first shot struck the door behind him. He dropped to one knee as two more shots went over his head and shattered the glass of the door.

Clint drew his gun, but couldn't locate the source of the shooting. He stood up, stuck his arm through the broken glass, and unlocked the door from the inside. He ducked into the store and closed the door behind him as more lead struck it . . .

He went to the back door and looked out. No sign of any soldiers. Out front he could hear the firing continue, as hot lead wreaked havoc on the interior.

He opened the door and stepped out into the dark alley behind the store. Quickly he ran along the back of the building. He came to an alley that would lead him to the street, but that wasn't his goal. His goal was to get to San Francisco in one piece. Apparently, someone didn't want him to make the trip . . .

## DON'T MISS THESE
## ALL-ACTION WESTERN SERIES
## FROM THE BERKLEY PUBLISHING GROUP

### THE GUNSMITH by J. R. Roberts
Clint Adams was a legend among lawmen, outlaws, and ladies. They called him . . . the Gunsmith.

### LONGARM by Tabor Evans
The popular long-running series about Deputy U.S. Marshal Custis Long—his life, his loves, his fight for justice.

### SLOCUM by Jake Logan
Today's longest-running action Western. John Slocum rides a deadly trail of hot blood and cold steel.

### BUSHWHACKERS by B. J. Lanagan
An action-packed series by the creators of Longarm! The rousing adventures of the most brutal gang of cutthroats ever assembled—Quantrill's Raiders.

### DIAMONDBACK by Guy Brewer
Dex Yancey is Diamondback, a Southern gentleman turned con man when his brother cheats him out of the family fortune. Ladies love him. Gamblers hate him. But nobody pulls one over on Dex . . .

### WILDGUN by Jack Hanson
The blazing adventures of mountain man Will Barlow—from the creators of Longarm!

### TEXAS TRACKER by Tom Calhoun
J.T. Law: the most relentless—and dangerous—manhunter in all Texas. Where sheriffs and posses fail, he's the best man to bring in the most vicious outlaws—for a price.

# THE GUNSMITH

## ANDERSONVILLE VENGEANCE

## J. R. ROBERTS

JOVE BOOKS, NEW YORK

**THE BERKLEY PUBLISHING GROUP**
**Published by the Penguin Group**
**Penguin Group (USA) Inc.**
**375 Hudson Street, New York, New York 10014, USA**
Penguin Group (Canada), 90 Eglinton Avenue East, Suite 700, Toronto, Ontario M4P 2Y3, Canada
(a division of Pearson Penguin Canada Inc.)
Penguin Books Ltd., 80 Strand, London WC2R 0RL, England
Penguin Group Ireland, 25 St. Stephen's Green, Dublin 2, Ireland (a division of Penguin Books Ltd.)
Penguin Group (Australia), 250 Camberwell Road, Camberwell, Victoria 3124, Australia
(a division of Pearson Australia Group Pty. Ltd.)
Penguin Books India Pvt. Ltd., 11 Community Centre, Panchsheel Park, New Delhi—110 017, India
Penguin Group (NZ), 67 Apollo Drive, Rosedale, North Shore 0632, New Zealand
(a division of Pearson New Zealand Ltd.)
Penguin Books (South Africa) (Pty.) Ltd., 24 Sturdee Avenue, Rosebank, Johannesburg 2196,
South Africa

Penguin Books Ltd., Registered Offices: 80 Strand, London WC2R 0RL, England

This is a work of fiction. Names, characters, places, and incidents either are the product of the author's imagination or are used fictitiously, and any resemblance to actual persons, living or dead, business establishments, events, or locales is entirely coincidental.

ANDERSONVILLE VENGEANCE

A Jove Book / published by arrangement with the author

PRINTING HISTORY
Jove edition / November 2010

ISBN: 978-0-515-14856-5

JOVE®
Jove Books are published by The Berkley Publishing Group,
a division of Penguin Group (USA) Inc.,
375 Hudson Street, New York, New York 10014.
JOVE® is a registered trademark of Penguin Group (USA) Inc.
The "J" design is a trademark of Penguin Group (USA) Inc.

PRINTED IN THE UNITED STATES OF AMERICA

10  9  8  7  6  5  4  3  2  1

# ONE

Clint Adams rarely went back to Atlanta. There were no good memories there. Not one. The only thing that was there was pain.

As he stepped off the train, the pain came back—not as sharply, but as a dull thing eating at his insides. But he knew that if he allowed it to, it would become sharp, start digging at his insides until he couldn't stand it anymore. He was determined not to let that happen.

The summons that had brought him to Atlanta had come from the only man who could have brought him back there—James West.

He walked down the platform to the stock car just as they were leading Eclipse down the ramp.

"I'll take him," he said, accepting the reins. "Thanks."

He walked Eclipse off the platform and headed into Atlanta. The town had grown by leaps and bounds since being reconstructed after Sherman's fiery march. It was a full-fledged city now, but a city he didn't know and he didn't intend to know.

He'd agreed to have a meeting at a hotel near the train

station. He walked Eclipse to a livery stable, where he left him in the hands of a black man who worked there. The man's skin was smooth and ashy, his hair gray. He could have been sixty or seventy, but he was still tall and powerfully built, with hands that had been nipped at and damaged from years of dealing with horses.

"I'll take good care of him, mister," the man said.

"I know you will. Thanks."

With his saddlebags and rifle, Clint walked to the agreed-upon meeting place, the Peach Blossom Hotel. He entered the lobby, which was filled with wicker furniture and vases of peach blossoms.

"Can we help you, suh?" the clerk asked with a syrupy Southern accent. He was a bright-faced man in his early thirties.

"Room," Clint said. "My name is Adams."

"Ah, yes, Mr. Adams," the man said, his face brightening even more. "We've been expectin' you. Would you sign the register, please?"

Clint did so, then accepted his key from the clerk.

"Any messages for me?" Clint asked.

"Uh, no, sir," the clerk said. "No messages."

"Okay, thanks."

"Do you need any help—"

"This is all I have," Clint said, indicating his rifle and saddlebags. "I'm fine."

"Yes, sir."

Clint nodded to the clerk and went up to his room on the second floor.

In his room he found the same wicker furniture, and a comfortable-looking bed. He knew there were hotels in Atlanta with indoor plumbing and electricity, but this wasn't one of them. A pitcher and basin sat on the dresser, and a gas lamp hung on the wall next to the door.

He dropped his saddlebags on the bed, propped the rifle

in a corner. Then he walked to the window and looked out. He could see the train station from there. He wished he was getting back on the train.

His meeting wasn't with James West. His friend was on a mission, which was usually the case. Instead, he would be meeting with someone from his past, Colonel Frederick Tate. When he had last seen Tate, the soldier had been a lieutenant, and his commanding officer.

Clint gave very little thought to the role he played in the war, and he did that by design. He had trained himself not to think back to that time. It was only at West's behest that he was allowing himself to be drawn back there.

He didn't know when the meeting with the colonel was supposed to take place. Certainly within the next few days, but West's telegram had not been any more precise than that. Clint had to register at the hotel and wait to be contacted.

Suddenly, he was hungry. Walking through the lobby, he had noticed there was a small restaurant right off it. That was good. He wouldn't have to go very far to get something to eat.

He went to his saddlebags, opened them, and took out his Colt New Line. His intention was to take off his gun belt and just carry the smaller gun, but in the end he stuffed it back into the bag, turned, and left the room still wearing his Colt. Clint had an edible steak and some weak coffee in the hotel dining room. On his way back through the lobby the clerk waved to him.

"I do have a message for you, Mr. Adams," the man said. "Came in while you were eating."

Clint accepted the envelope and asked, "Who brought it in?"

"It was a soldier, sir," the man said. "A private."

"Okay, thank you."

Clint took the message to his room, but he didn't read it until he was behind closed doors.

The message was from Colonel Frederick Tate, asking Clint to meet him at an address that evening at 10 p.m. Although the clerk said the message was brought by a soldier, Clint had to wonder if it was legitimate. Why wouldn't the colonel simply come to the hotel to see him?

He decided he'd keep the appointment, but he was going to be real careful while doing it.

# TWO

The address he'd been given was not far away, in a neighborhood of shops, stores, and restaurants. However, since it was late at night, most of those places were closed. All of their doorways were dark, perfect places for a gunman to lie in wait.

The address in question looked like a general store, with a small café on one side and a ladies' hat shop on the other. All were dark.

Clint stood across the street from the place, using one of those darkened doorways himself to observe the area for a while. He was looking for telltale signs that someone was hiding—the scuff of a shoe, the momentary flare of a cigarette being lit, or smoked. When he was reasonably satisfied that no one was waiting for him, he broke from his doorway and crossed to the store. He paused a moment to look over his shoulder at the rooftops across the street, then stepped up to the door and knocked. After a moment he heard footsteps, then someone pushed the curtain in the window aside and peered out. The lock was disengaged, and the door opened.

"Mr. Adams?" a man asked.

"That's right."

"Come in, sir," the man said.

He wore a blue uniform, and was a private. No doubt the man who had delivered the message. As Clint entered, the soldier stuck his head out, looked around, then pulled back in and closed the door, locking it.

"This way, sir."

"Whoa, Private," Clint said. "How about you identify yourself?"

"Sorry, sir," the man said. He was not young, in his thirties, slight but sturdy. "I'm Private Collins, sir, assigned to Colonel Tate's staff."

"I see. Is Tate here?"

"Yes, sir," the private said. "He's in the back, waiting for you."

"All right, then, Private," Clint said. "Lead the way."

"Yes, sir," Collins said. "This way."

He started back and Clint followed. Collins led Clint through the store to a back door, which normally led to a storeroom. As they went through the door, Clint saw that it was, indeed, a storeroom, but there was more than merchandise stored there.

They had to go down a flight of stairs to reach the floor of the storage area, and then someone turned up the gas on a lamp and lit the room.

In the center of the room, in full uniform, was Colonel Frederick Tate. He had filled out since Clint had seen him last, fuller in the shoulders and chest than he had been twenty years before. He had also acquired a full beard, which was peppered with gray.

"Clint Adams."

"Colonel," Clint said. "Good to see you."

Clint walked to Tate and extended his hand. The two men shook warmly.

"It's been a long time," Tate said.

"Yes, sir, it has."

"Camp Sumter seems a long time ago," Tate said, "and yet it's so vivid in my mind."

"It would be in mine, too, sir, if I allowed it to be."

"I understand," Tate said. "I wish I could block it out, but I can't."

Clint nodded.

"Private, a chair for Mr. Adams."

"Yes, sir."

Collins came forward and put a wooden chair down for Clint. There was already one for the colonel, and they both sat.

"That's all, Private," Tate said. "Keep an eye on the front."

"Yes, sir."

Colonel Tate was obviously waiting for Private Collins to leave before he spoke again, so Clint remained silent and waited.

"Anybody covering the back?" Clint asked.

"Two of my men. Were you worried this might be some kind of trap?"

"I was."

"But you came anyway."

"Well, Jim West's name and yours were connected to the telegram I got," Clint said. "How could I not come?"

"I appreciate that, Clint," Tate said. "Do you have any idea what this is about?"

"Well, considering your involvement, and the fact that we're in Atlanta," Clint said, "I figured it has to do with Camp Sumter."

"I hate to say it," Colonel Frederick Tate said, "but it does have everything to do with Andersonville."

# THREE

## CAMP SUMTER—ANDERSONVILLE, GEORGIA
## SUMMER 1864

There were two ways into Camp Sumter—called Andersonville by most—the south entrance and the north entrance. Clint Adams was among the new prisoners being walked in through the north gate.

What greeted the new prisoners was appalling. Men—formally fighting men—who had now been reduced to walking skeletons, covered with dirt and insects.

"Can this be hell?" the man next to Clint asked.

"Looks like it," he said.

In the center of the camp was a swamp, which was obviously used as the camp latrine. Human excrement overflowed from it, and the smell was so intense it was almost like a solid well. Clint's eyes and those of the men around him immediately began to tear.

"My God!" one of them said, covering his mouth and nose.

"Easy, solider," Clint said.

The twelve men being marched in with Clint were soldiers. He was a civilian, working for E. J. Allen's Secret Service.

"How do they expect us to live through this?" another man asked. "It's summer, for Chrissake. We're all gonna get the plague."

"That's probably just what they want," Clint said.

Confederate soldiers marched them to their barracks, which were little more than chicken coops.

"Inside," one of the soldiers said.

"Where's the superior officer of the Union prisoners?" Clint demanded. "I want to see him."

The gray coat grinned at him and said, "Then do what I tol' you, blue-belly. Get inside."

Clint waited for the soldiers to file inside and then followed.

"Any superior officers among you?" someone asked.

"No, sir," Clint said. "All enlisted men, and me."

"You? What are you if not an enlisted man or a superior officer?"

"Civilian, sir."

A young man approached him, stared at him intently. The remnants of his blue coat identified him as a lieutenant.

"Spy?" he asked in a low voice.

"Civilian," Clint said again.

"I understand," the man said." I'm Lieutenant Tate. I'm ranking here."

"No one higher?"

"We had a captain, but he died yesterday. I thought there might be someone with you."

"No," Clint said. "You're still ranking."

Clint looked around, tried to see in the semidarkness of the coop. There were men lying on men, and the men who had come in with him were trying to avoid them. Some of them might have been dead, it was hard to tell.

"I know what you're thinking," the lieutenant said. "Sometimes we don't know who's dead and who's alive until they have us file out in the morning."

"This is inhuman," Clint said.

"Exactly."

"Is there water?"

"There's a creek that runs through the camp," Tate said. "It's used to bathe in, and for drinking water."

"It must be polluted by now," Clint said.

"I'm sure it is," Tate said, "but it's all the water we've got."

"How long have you been here?" Clint asked.

"Not as long as most of these poor wretches," Tate said.

Clint could see the man was thin, but not yet emaciated.

"I'm still fairly healthy," Tate said. "So are the men who came in with me. Those who were here before us aren't as lucky. That is, except for the Raiders."

"Raiders?"

"The Andersonville Raiders, we call them," Tate said. "They kill and steal from other prisoners."

"Prisoners killing prisoners?" Clint asked. "With what as weapons?"

"Clubs, bare hands, anything they can get their hands on," Tate said. "We pretty much have to stick together to avoid them. If they catch you alone, or even in twos, they'll attack."

"Jesus," Clint said. "That's what we've been reduced to?"

"Some of us."

Clint and Tate moved to the entrance of the coop.

"Anyone escaped?" Clint asked.

"No."

"Anyone try?"

"Oh, yes. No one's ever gotten past the dead line."

"The dead line?"

"See the light fence? That's the 'dead line.' It's about

three feet inside the stockade. Anyone trying to cross those three feet is shot. No one's ever made it to the wall."

"And if they did?"

"It's made of heavy, sixteen-foot logs. A healthy man like you would have trouble scaling it. Once you've been here awhile, there's no chance."

Clint looked out at other coops, like the one he was in. The smell of the marsh in the center was still there, though not as strong.

"Are the Raiders all bunked together?" he asked.

"No," Tate said. "There are some in each barracks."

"Why don't you form a group to stop them?"

"Well," Tate said, "up to yesterday I wasn't in charge."

"Now you are," Clint said.

"What's your name?" Tate asked.

"Clint Adams."

Tate looked more closely at him.

"I've heard of you," he said, "but I didn't know you were so young."

"I don't think age makes much difference in here, Lieutenant," Clint said. "Do you?"

"No, Mr. Adams," Tate said, "I don't."

"Well," Clint said, "why don't we see what we can do about those Raiders?"

# FOUR

Colonel Tate stood up, reached behind a box, and came out with a bottle of whiskey and two glasses. He poured the two glasses and handed one to Clint, then sat back down.

"To the dead of Andersonville," he said.

Clint lifted his glass, and they both drank.

"Henry Wirz," Tate said.

"Commandant of Camp Sumter," Clint said. "He was hanged in 1865."

"Was he?"

Clint stared.

"Wasn't he?" Clint asked. "He was tried by General Wallace, prosecuted by Norton Chipman, and many of us testified against him, including you and me."

"Did you see him hang?" Tate asked.

"No, I wasn't present at the execution."

"Neither was I."

"Sir, are you telling me he wasn't executed?"

"That's not exactly what I'm saying, Clint," Tate replied.

"Then what are you saying, sir?"

"Have another drink."

Tate reached out with the bottle and filled Clint's glass, then his own.

"There's a report that Wirz was seen, alive," Tate said.

"Where did that report come from?"

"San Francisco."

"And who saw him?"

"Atwater."

"Dorence Atwater?"

"That's right."

At Camp Sumter, Atwater was a young Union soldier who had been tasked with keeping a record of the names of the dead. When the prisoners of Andersonville were expatriated, his list was suppressed until he got it to Horace Greeley of *The New York Times*.

"Dorence Atwater saw Henry Wirz in San Francisco?" Clint asked, to make it clear to himself.

"Or thinks he did."

"Have you talked to Atwater?"

Tate shook his head.

"Telegram. Have you seen Atwater since the war?" Tate asked.

"No, sir."

"He's worked as a journalist for a variety of different newspapers."

"*The Times*?"

"No, never," Tate said. "Small newspapers."

"How old is he now?"

"He's . . . in his early forties."

"And working in San Francisco now?"

"As far as we know."

"Why not just bring him in?" Clint asked. "To Washington? And talk to him?"

"He won't come in," Tate said. "He says he's going to kill Wirz."

"Wirz is dead."

"Not according to Atwater."

"Then he's going to kill an innocent man."

"Not according to him," Tate said. "The man he says is Wirz is Harlan Winston."

"Senator Harlan Winston?"

"That's right."

"He's protected, isn't he?"

"He is," Tate said, "but he's not invulnerable. Atwater is determined to kill him."

"So stop him."

"We want you to stop him."

"Why me?"

"He knows you."

"He knows you, too."

"He trusts you," Tate said. "He trusted you in Andersonville."

"That doesn't mean he'll trust me now."

"Do you trust me?"

"Yes."

"Why?"

"Because I trusted you in Andersonville."

"And I trusted you," Tate said. "And that's why I want you for this job."

Clint held out his glass for another finger of whiskey.

"Will you do it?"

"Save the senator, stop Atwater, bring him back . . . ?" Clint asked.

"All three."

Clint drank his whiskey.

"Sure," he said, "why not? What else have I got to do?"

Clint stood up.

"When do I leave?" he asked.

"There's a train to Saint Louis in the morning," Tate said. "There you'll board a private military train. It'll take you the rest of the way."

"All the way to San Francisco?"

Tate nodded. "That's right. What will you need?"

"My horse, my gear."

"Be at the train station at eight a.m.," Tate said.

"Yes, sir."

"And thank you, Clint."

"Of course, sir."

"Keep in touch by telegraph."

"To Washington?"

"Yes."

"All right."

He started for the door.

"Clint?"

"Yes."

"You knew Wirz."

"You know I did."

"Then you'll recognize him."

"After all these years?" Clint asked. "Maybe. Except for one thing."

"What's that?"

"Henry Wirz is dead."

"Well, then," Tate said, "that's the other thing you'll have to do."

"What?"

"Confirm."


Private Collins let Clint out the front door, closed, and locked it behind him. Clint stood for a moment with his back to the door. Going in, he'd felt sure of himself.

Going out, he felt bad.

Very bad.

# FIVE

## CAMP SUMTER, 1864

Clint was shoved into the room. Weakened from his first month in Andersonville, he stumbled and fell to the floor. From there he looked up at the man in front of him.

"I am Major Heinrich Hartmann Wirz," the man said. "Henry Wirz."

"I know who you are."

"Yes, and I know who you are," Wirz said. He was in his forties, a slight man with a useless right arm. "Clint Adams. I understand they call you the Gunsmith."

"So?"

"Is that true?" Wirz asked. "You are a gunsmith?"

Wirz apparently did not understand the true genesis of the name. Clint wasn't inclined to tell him.

"Yes," Clint said, "I'm a gunsmith."

"Good," Wirz said with a slight accent. It was Swiss, which Clint did not know at the time. "I need a gunsmith to work on my men's weapons."

"Why should I do that?"

"Why, for extra rations, of course."

"More slop?" Clint asked. "No thank you."

"Well, then, do it so that I will not kill any of your Regulators."

"Regulators?"

"Do not take me for a fool, Adams," Wirz said. "You have formed a group of Regulators to defend against the group you call 'the Andersonville Raiders.' Is that not so?"

"Yes, it is."

"Then if you do not work on my guns, I will kill one of your Regulators each day, starting with Lieutenant Tate."

"You can't kill our superior officer."

"He will die of an accident," Wirz said. "Or perhaps of natural causes."

Clint thought fast.

"Let's make a deal," he said.

"What do you propose?"

"Decent food, clean water."

"For your Regulators?"

"For all the men."

"Impossible. I will supply what you ask only for your Regulators. It will keep their strength up in order to deal with the Raiders who have, I believe, superior numbers."

"That's true, they do."

"Then you will have superior conditioning," Wirz said. "Accept these terms, or we will return to my original offer. I will kill a Regulator each day, beginning with your Lieutenant Tate."

"All right," Clint said. "All right, I'll work on your guns in return for food and water for the Regulators. All of them."

"Very well," Wirz said. "How many of them are there?"

There were half a dozen, but Clint said, "Twenty."

# SIX

The first shot struck the door behind him. He dropped to one knee as two more shots went over his head and shattered the glass of the door.

Clint drew his gun, but couldn't locate the source of the shooting. He stood up, stuck his arm through the broken glass, and unlocked the door from the inside. He ducked into the store and closed the door behind him as more lead struck it.

He looked around inside. No sign of Private Collins. He hurried through the store to the storeroom, down the stairs. The lamp was still burning, but there was no sign of Collins or Tate. They must have left immediately.

He went to the back door and looked out. No sign of any soldiers. Out front he could hear the firing continue, as hot lead wreaked havoc on the interior.

He opened the door and stepped out into the dark alley behind the store. Quickly he ran along the back of the building. He came to an alley that would lead him to the street, but that wasn't his goal. His goal was to get to San Francisco in one piece. Apparently, someone didn't want him to make the trip. But he was sure hired gunmen were out front doing the shooting. He could have made his way to the street and taken them on, but that wasn't his intention.

He had to get away, just as Colonel Tate and his men had done.

Clint continued to move along behind buildings until he was far enough away from the store. The shooting had either stopped, or he was too far away to hear it. They probably knew by now that he was gone.

He found his way to the street and retraced his steps back to his hotel. Across the street from the Peach Blossom Hotel he stopped to take a look. He heard something to his right, turned, and drew his gun. A girl stepped from the darkness. She had a shawl covering her head, but he could see she had big brown eyes.

"Don't go in there," she said. "They're waitin' for you."

"Who is?" he asked.

"Men with guns."

"How do you know?"

"Because I've been waitin' for you, too," she said.

He holstered his gun.

"Why?"

"To save you, of course," she said. "Come this way."

"Where are you taking me?"

"Someplace safe," she said.

She started to walk and he hesitated. She looked at him over her shoulder.

"If I wanted to harm you," she said, "I would have let you walk in there."

She had a point.

"What's your name?"

"That can come later. Come on."

"Tell me now," he said. "So I know who I'm going with."

"My name is Molly. Now will you come?"

"My name is Clint."

"Follow me, Clint," she said, "and you'll live to tell me your last name."

He followed.

# SEVEN

Clint followed the girl through the dark streets of Atlanta until they came to a stop in front of a modest two-story house.

"Who lives here?" he asked.

"It's a rooming house," Molly said.

"You have a room here?"

"No, you do."

"I have a room at the hotel—"

"Which you can't go back to, or you'll be killed," she said.

"My stuff is in my room—"

"Your saddlebags and rifle are here," she said.

"How did that happen?"

"I moved them."

"By whose okay?"

"On my own initiative."

"And my horse?"

"Also moved someplace safe."

He was surprised.

"Now who accomplished that without losing a finger?" he asked.

"I did," she said. "I have a way with males—horses or humans."

"Hmm."

"Do you want to go inside?" she asked. "It's safe, and you can get some rest before catching your train tomorrow."

"What do you know about me catching a train?"

"I know everything about it," she said, "but do you really want to talk about it out here? On the street?"

She had a point.

"No, I don't."

"Then let's go inside."

She went up the steps to the front door and he followed. She used a key to get in, then led him up a flight of stairs to the second floor.

"Isn't there anyone else staying here?" he whispered.

"Not right now," she said, "so there's no need to whisper."

"The house is empty?"

"I thought that would be best."

"Don't tell me, let me guess," he said in his normal tone. "You own the house."

"No," she said, "my aunt does."

She led him to a door, opened it, and stepped inside. She struck a match and lit a lamp that was sitting on a dresser. It lit the room well, showing him a fourposter, the dresser the lamp was on, and a wooden chair with arms and a cushion.

He looked at the girl, who removed the shawl from her head and let it rest on her shoulders. Wavy brown curls fell to her shoulder and he saw how pretty she really was. Big, wide brown eyes, a snub nosed covered by freckles, and a wide, full-lipped mouth.

"Irish?" he asked.

"Through and through," she said. "Is that a problem?"

"Not for me."

She removed the shawl from her shoulders and dropped it on the bed, next to his saddlebags. He saw his rifle leaning against the wall in a corner. She was wearing a very simple blue cotton dress that fit her well enough to show the curves of her body.

"Are you injured?" she asked.

"No," he said. "Why would I be?"

"When somebody shoots at you, sometimes you get hurt," she said.

"How do you know I was shot at?"

"I was there, Mr. Adams," she said. "I saw and heard the shots."

"I guess my question is, why were you there?" he asked. "And why were you outside my hotel? And why did you move me here?"

"So your question is pretty much, why?"

"That's it."

"The answer is easy," she said. "It's my job."

"Your job?" he asked. "Do you work for Colonel Tate?"

"No, I'm not military," she said. "I work for the Secret Service. Like your friend, Jim West. He asked me to help you, if I could."

"Jim sent you?"

"Is that so hard to believe?" she asked, putting her hands on her hips. She stood about five-four, was built solidly. "That Jim would trust a woman?"

"Not at all," Clint said. "I've learned over the years to trust Jim's instincts."

"Well, he has a little more than instinct to base his confidence on," she said. "We've worked together before."

Clint studied her for a moment.

"I wouldn't have known about your meeting with the colonel if I wasn't on the inside," she told him. "There's no need to suspect me."

"I'm just careful," he said.

"No harm in that, I guess," she said. "You should be safe here tonight."

"Where will you be?"

"I'll be downstairs," she said.

"On guard?"

"Sure," she said. "That way you can get some sleep."

"I'm not used to being watched over by a woman," he said.

"Any objections?"

"None."

"Don't worry," she said, "I'm armed and I know how to use a gun."

"That's comforting."

She pushed out her pretty jaw and asked, "Is that sarcasm?"

"Not at all," he said. "I'm too tired to be sarcastic. I appreciate your help, Molly."

"Well," she said, "okay, then. I'll, uh, see you in the morning. I'll make sure you make your eight a.m. train."

"Thanks, again."

She nodded, headed for the door.

"You mind if I ask your last name?"

"It's Molly O'Henry."

"Miss?"

"Yes."

"Thank you, Miss O'Henry."

"You're welcome, Mr. Adams."

As she opened the door, he said, "I thought you said you needed me to tell you my last name."

"I lied," she said. "I know everything there is to know about you."

"Everything?"

She gave him a long look before closing the door behind her, and said, "Everything."

# EIGHT

Clint walked to the window after Molly had left and stared down at the area in front of the house. Somebody knew he was meeting with the colonel, and had tried to ambush him. But why wait until he had gone inside? Why not try to kill him before?

Or why try to kill him at all?

It was highly unlikely that Henry Wirz was still alive. It was more likely that Dorence Atwater—who had been a very young man when he was in Andersonville—was mistaken. Maybe he was still looking for some justice after Andersonville.

But if it wasn't Wirz, who had sent the gunmen after him tonight?

And why hadn't Jim West or Colonel Tate told him about Molly O'Henry? He had only the young woman's word that she was with the Secret Service. True, she knew about his meeting with Tate, but then so did the gunmen who'd tried to kill him.

He had only one way to get in touch with Tate again, and that was the same telegraph address he'd responded to in the first place. Apparently, it went to a telegraph key in Washington.

He walked to the bed, hung his gun belt on the bedpost, but kept his boots on. Molly had told him he was safe there, but there was no telling. He didn't think he'd been followed from his meeting, or that they had been followed from the hotel, but he decided to play it safe by keeping the gun close, and the boots on.

He thought back to Andersonville, where he, Tate, and Atwater were members of the Regulators. The Raiders had been running rampant until Clint got there just as Tate became the superior officer in camp.

Atwater was barely old enough to be in the war and was mostly given paperwork to do. He kept records for them as to who died, who were Regulators, and who were Raiders. For one so young, Atwater had seemed to be very strong-minded while at Camp Sumter. Even after they were released, he did not suffer the same mental problems many of the other prisoners had.

At least, he didn't seem to. Perhaps it had been working on him for more than twenty years, until now he was seeing Henry Wirz's face when he looked at the face of Senator Harlan Winston.

Hmmm.

He thought a moment.

Henry Wirz.

Harlan Winston.

Even if Wirz had been Winston, wouldn't he have been smart enough to change his initials? Clint knew that outlaws and ex-cons very often kept the same initials when they changed their names. Supposedly, it made the alias easier to remember.

But Wirz had been nothing if not an intelligent officer. Surely he would have been sharper than that when it came to choosing a phony name.

But Wirz was dead. He had to be. He'd been tried, convicted, and ultimately, executed. Hanged. In front of witnesses.

But who were the witnesses?

He wondered if he sent a telegram to the colonel in Washington if the man would send him a list of the witnesses to Henry Wirz's execution?

He placed his hands behind his neck and stared at the ceiling. He only became aware of the fact that he had fallen asleep when there was a knock at the door, waking him.

Molly went downstairs and immediately went to the back door. She opened it and let Colonel Frederick Tate into the kitchen.

"Is he all right?" Tate asked, keeping his voice low.

"He wasn't injured."

"Did he believe Jim West sent you?"

"He seems to."

"All right," Tate said. "Just get him to the train station tomorrow."

"What if someone tries to kill him there?" she asked.

"Keep him alive."

"Why can't you do it . . . sir?"

"I can't have soldiers at the station," Tate said. "I need you there, Molly."

"All right, I'll do it," Molly said.

"Stay close to him," Tate said. "Stay real close."

"I understand," she said. "Close."

She let him out the kitchen door, then locked it and went into the living room. She had intended to go to her "aunt's" bedroom and get some sleep, but thought it best to stay in the living room, on watch.

She sat on the sofa, started thinking about everything she had heard about Clint Adams. She drifted off to sleep, then awoke with a start. She needed to stay alert. She could either make coffee, or . . .

# NINE

Clint walked to the door, gun in hand, even though it could have been only one person.

Molly.

"Can I come in?" she asked.

"Sure."

He backed away, allowed her to enter, then holstered the gun.

"What's on your mind?" he asked.

"To be frank," she said, "you."

"What about me?"

She looked down.

"You sleep with your boots on?"

"Only when somebody's trying to kill me."

"I told you, you're safe here."

"With you."

She hesitated, then said, "Maybe."

"What do you mean, maybe?"

"I was downstairs, thinking about everything I know about you."

"And?"

"West told me about you."

"Oh."

"So I was thinking, if I fall asleep downstairs, I can't watch over you."

"You were falling asleep?"

"Drifting off," she said. "That's when I started thinking."

"About me."

"Uh-huh."

"I haven't been with a man in . . . months," she said. "And even then it wasn't good."

"How old are you?"

"Twenty-eight."

"You don't look it."

"I've been with men, Adams," she said. "A lot of men. And you've been with a lot of women . . . by all accounts."

"I've been at it a little longer than you have," he said.

"Granted."

He sat on the bed.

"So what's on your mind?"

"I told you," she said.

"Me," Clint said. "Sex with me?"

"Yes."

"Just like that?"

"According to Jim West," she said, "you have sex with women, just like that."

"Sometimes."

"What's wrong with me?" she asked.

"I don't trust you."

She touched the neck of her dress, brought her hand down over her breasts.

"You have to trust me to sleep with me?"

"Probably not."

She came over and sat next to him on the bed, her shoulder touching his.

"I'll bet you don't even have to like a woman to sleep with her."

"It helps, though."

"Do you like me?"

"I don't dislike you," he said. "But I haven't known you long enough to know if I actually like you."

"Look," she said, "it'll keep us both awake."

"I thought the point was for me to get some sleep," he said.

"Okay," she said, putting her hand on his thigh, "it'll help us both sleep better."

He looked at her, lowered his eyes. The dress was thin, and he could see that her nipples were hard. They were also large. He found himself wondering what color they were.

And that did it.

"Okay," he said, "that's an argument I can accept."

# TEN

Clint knelt down in front of Molly and peeled off her dress. The top slopes of her breasts were covered with freckles. He went slow, bringing her nipples into sight eventually, and was pleased to see how brown they were.

"What are you . . . smiling at?" she asked, her breath catching when he touched one of her nipples with the tip of his right forefinger.

"I had a bet with myself they'd be brown," he said.

"You won."

"Yes," he said, "I certainly did."

He took her breasts in his hands and squeezed them, using his thumbs to flick her nipples. Her breath caught again.

"You know," she said, "I thought I wanted to come in here and have you tear my clothes off and throw me down on the bed."

"But?"

"But I think I like this better."

"Sometimes," he said, "slow is better."

He leaned in and kissed her breasts, then went to work

getting the dress the rest of the way off her. She lifted her butt off the bed to help, and then she was naked.

"Very nice," he said.

"Thank you," she said. "But I believe now it's your turn."

"I might need some help with my boots."

She grinned, stood up, and knelt down in front of her. He sat on the bed and the naked girl helped him off with his boots, her breasts jiggling with the effort. Next, she undid his belt and trousers, slid them down to his ankles, where he kicked them away. He pulled his shirt off himself, then lifted his butt off the bed to help her slide his underwear off.

And then, too, he was naked.

"Oh my," she said as his cock jutted up from his crotch.

She slid her left hand beneath his testicles and cradled them, slid the right hand up his cock, stroking it slowly.

"Come up here—" he said thickly, reaching for her.

"Uh-uh," she said, using her left hand to swat him away. "Sometimes it's better to go slow, remember?"

"Who said that?"

"You did."

She swooped down on him with her mouth, took him inside. She was right. She was experienced, and good. She moaned as she sucked him avidly, sliding up and down on him wetly. She put her hand on his chest and pushed him down onto his back. She burrowed down into his crotch, lifted his testicles, and licked underneath them. Then she licked her way up his hard cock and took him into her mouth again. She sucked him until he was only moments away from exploding, then released him and used her hand to stop him.

"Jesus," he said.

"Good?" she asked.

"Better than good," he said.

She slid up on top of him, rubbed herself against him. Her pussy was wet as she slid it up and down the length of his penis. He enjoyed the feel on not only her slick pussy lips, but the wiry black hair that surrounded it. She continued to rub herself against him like a cat, until he asserted himself, grabbed her, and flipped her over on her back.

He slid his hand down between her legs while kissing and licking her breasts, sucking her nipples, biting her neck. She moaned and writhed beneath his touch as his fingers probed and poked her. Slowly, he kissed his way down her sturdy body until his face was pressed to her pubic patch. He rubbed her hair over his face, inhaling the heady scent of her, and then finally licking her, slowly running his tongue up and down her, and then in and out of her.

"Oh, Jesus . . ." she said, lifting her hips to meet the pressure of his tongue, reaching down to hold his head so he couldn't get away from her.

Getting away was the last thing on his mind. He burrowed his tongue into her, used his lips, his chin, did everything he could to drive her into a frenzy on the bed.

When he felt she could take no more, he mounted her and drove his rigid cock into her. She caught her breath and her body went taut. She spread her legs, opening herself as wide as she could to him, finally grabbing hold of her own ankles. He took her like that, slamming in and out of her as hard as he could, and it was a good thing the house was empty.

Or was it?

# ELEVEN

They were lying side by side sometime later, both sweating from their exertions, when suddenly Clint stiffened.

"What?" she asked.

"Shh," he said. "I thought I heard something."

They both listened intently, heard floorboards creaking.

"Somebody's downstairs," he said.

"That can't be," she said. "Nobody knows about this place."

"Somebody does. Where's your gun?"

Angry with herself, she said, "I left it downstairs."

He sat up, swinging his feet to the floor.

"Get dressed," he said, pulling on his trousers and grabbing his gun.

He walked to the door of the room and cracked it open. Holding his gun, he listened while Molly slipped back into her dress.

"Does your aunt have any weapons up here?" he asked.

"There is no aunt," she said. "I own this house, under a phony name. That's why I said nobody knows about it. My gun is in the bedroom downstairs."

"Is there a back way down?"

"No," she said, "but I can lower myself from this window to the ground, and then get into my bedroom from the window below."

"All right," he said, "but wait until I get out into the hall. How long will you need?"

"Five minutes, that's all."

"Okay," he said, "in five minutes you come out of your bedroom with your gun ready. I'll come down the stairs."

"What if they come up first?"

"Then I'll meet them in the hall."

She looked at him, then smiled.

"My legs are a little weak."

He grinned and said, "Mine, too."

She went to the window and quietly opened it.

"Five minutes," he said, and she nodded.

He slipped out of the room.

# TWELVE

Clint closed the door behind him and moved quietly down the hall. At least, he tried to move quietly, but even he could hear the floorboards creaking beneath his own feet.

He reached the top of the steps and stopped. He had to give Molly time to get herself into position.

Again, he could clearly hear the sound of movement on the first floor.

Molly had told a half-truth. There was an aunt, but she was long dead. She had often snuck out of her bedroom in her aunt's house this way in her youth, hanging from the edge of the window and then dropping down to the garden below. Her aunt always knew, because Molly used to trample the flowers in the garden when she did this. But the garden was long dead—like her aunt—and as she dropped down, she landed on bare dirt. She paused, waiting to see if anyone had heard her.

Satisfied that she had gone undetected, she silently opened the window to what was now her own bedroom, slid over the sill into the room. Again, she paused and listened, then moved.

She had left her gun on the dresser top. It was still there, a .32 caliber Colt Paterson. She picked it up and checked it quickly to make sure it was loaded, then went to the door. She listened first, then opened it a crack. By her reckoning there was one minute left . . .

Clint figured Molly would be in place by now. He only hoped she was as good with a gun as she was in bed.

He started down the stairs, but he did it on the run. Trying to go down quietly would never have worked. He'd noticed how creaky they had been when they first went up, so sneaking down was out of the question.

He rushed down to the first floor, gun ready, and looked around.

No one.

Molly came rushing out of the back, her Colt in hand. She stopped short when she saw Clint standing there alone.

"Did you see anyone?" she asked.

"No."

"Could we have been wrong?"

He held his finger to his lips and pointed to the kitchen. Together they walked to the doorway and peered in. The room was empty, and the back door was open.

"We weren't wrong," he said. "Somebody was here, but they're gone."

"Why?" she asked. "What did they come for?"

"That's for you to discover," he said. "Let's light some lamps and see what we can see."

"First," she said, "I'll close and lock that door."

"It was closed and locked before, right?" he asked. "And somebody still got in."

"I'll close it anyway."

He watched her back while she closed the door, then lit a lamp in the kitchen. She looked around.

"I don't see anything amiss here," she said.

"Stay away from the windows," Clint said. "There may be somebody outside. Let's check the other rooms."

They went into the living room and lit another lamp.

"Same here," she said. "Nothing."

"Are you sure?"

She looked around again, then frowned.

"That desk."

There was a small writing desk against one wall.

"What about it?"

She walked to it. There was a drawer in the center that was ajar.

"This drawer was closed."

"How do you know?"

"Because it's my desk, and I make sure I close all the drawers."

"What was in it?"

She opened it wide. There were papers there.

"Just some letters, and important papers."

"Are they all there?"

"Yes," she said, "but someone has riffled through them."

"Looking for what?"

"I don't know," she said.

"Your assignment?"

"I don't keep anything in writing that has to do with my job."

"Maybe they didn't know that."

Clint still had his gun in his hand. Now he tucked it into his belt.

"I think we better stay awake the rest of the night," he said.

"We could go back to your room," she said. "Or mine."

"By awake," he said, "I meant awake and alert."

"I could make some coffee, and something to eat," she said.

"That's a good start," he said. "There's still about seven hours before I have to make that train."

*"We,"* she said.

"What?"

*"We* have to make that train. I'm going with you to San Francisco," she said. "You'll need somebody to watch your back."

*"We'll* need to stay alert, then, Molly," he told her.

She grinned.

"I know. That means no hanky-panky. So it's good we got it out of the way."

"How about that coffee?" he asked.

"And I think I've got some cold chicken."

"Sounds good."

They adjourned to the kitchen.

# THIRTEEN

At seven-thirty the next morning Clint and Molly left for the train station. They picked up Clint's horse, Eclipse, but Molly was making the trip without a mount of her own.

"If I need a horse, I can find one when we get there," she said.

In the daylight they were able to see a set of footprints outside the house, further indication that someone had been inside. Possibly, the person—a man, by the look of the tracks—had heard them having sex upstairs and used the noise to cover a search of the premises. He then made his escape by the back door.

As they approached the station, they saw that several people were waiting to board the train. Clint walked Eclipse up onto the platform and down to where he knew the stock car would stop.

"You know any of these other people?" he asked, looking around them.

"No, I don't," she said.

"But you're local."

"That's true," she said, "but I doubt any of them are.

Besides, just because I'm local doesn't mean I know everyone in Atlanta."

"Who's your immediate superior?" he asked. "Colonel Tate?"

"Tate is not with the Service," she said. "I can't tell you who my boss is, Clint."

Clint wasn't sure just who was sitting at the head of the Secret Service these days. The Pinkertons were no longer involved—he knew that. Allan had died, and his sons Robert and William were running the Pinkerton Detective Agency.

"But do you know Tate?"

"I've met him."

"I haven't seen him in years," Clint said. "Not since Andersonville."

Her eyes widened.

"You were in Andersonville?"

"Not for very long," he said, "and it's not something I tell people. In fact, I haven't told anyone before today."

"I'm flattered."

Clint noticed that two of the men waiting for the train were armed. One had a saddle slung over his shoulder. The other was wearing a gambler's black suit. Both had holsters on.

"We're going to have to watch those two," he said.

"Right," she said. "Maybe we should ride in the stock car, with your horse?"

"I don't think he'd like that," Clint said, patting Eclipse's neck. "He likes his space. No, we'll ride with the other passengers."

The sound of the train whistle interrupted them. Within minutes, the train was pulling into the station.

"Stand here," Clint said, moving Molly behind him.

"Why—you think somebody will use the noise of the train to shoot at us?"

He put his mouth to her ear and said, "The thought had crossed my mind."

But it didn't happen. When the stock car let down the ramp, Clint walked Eclipse onto the car himself. He took Molly with him. After making sure the Darley Arabian was secure, they walked back down, then made their way to the passenger car.

"I thought we were taking a private military train," she said when they were seated.

"Not from here," he said. "We'll pick it up in Saint Louis. Then we'll have a whole train to ourselves. For now, we have to be careful."

"I understand."

"Can you use that gun?"

She looked down at the gun in her holster.

"Yes."

"It's pretty small."

"It suits me. I can hit what I shoot at," she assured him.

"Okay," he said, "but don't shoot anybody unless I say so."

"I know my job, Clint."

"I'm sure you do," he said. "But you're here to assist me. I'm in command. Got it?"

She firmed her chin, suppressed what she was originally going to say, and instead replied, "I got it."

The train jerked, and then started forward.

"Good," he said.

He put his head back against the seat cushion and found himself drifting back to Andersonville . . .

# FOURTEEN

## CAMP SUMTER, 1865

The Regulators were originally looked upon as saviors in Andersonville. However, after Clint's deal with Henry Wirz to work on Confederate guns in return for water and food, Clint was looked upon by many of the prisoners as a traitor.

In truth, while there only six members in the Regulators, Clint had arranged for food for twenty men, and then divvied it up among more than fifty.

The men who didn't get the food and water were men who were beyond help, or members of the Andersonville Raiders.

Fortified by what little of the food and water they were actually consuming, Clint and the Regulators continued to combats the Raiders. Henry Wirz had been correct. While the Raiders were superior in numbers, the Regulators were superior in condition.

Clint, Tate, and the Regulators patrolled the camp at night. It was after dark when the Raiders usually hit. The Regulators were still trying to find out who the leaders of the Raiders were. If they could catch them, they were determined to try them in a prisoners' court.

As the Regulators patrolled at night, they carried whatever weapons they could find or fashion. Clint had a club he'd made from a thick tree branch he'd found near the polluted creek. He had used a sharp stone to trim the branches from it, and even strip the bark.

Tate carried a piece of wood he'd pulled free from the base of their barracks. It had a few nails sticking out the end, which he put to good use against Regulators.

Dorence Atwater patrolled with Clint and Tate, carrying a flat board he'd found somewhere, but he was not very much help in a fight, his specialty being paperwork. In his unit he had been the commanding officer's clerical worker. But he insisted on being part of the patrol.

On this particular night it was unbearably hot. Even though he had been eating somewhat better than most of the prisoners, Clint was still filthy, his clothes in tatters, his skin covered with lice and other insect bites. When he was first brought to the camp, his boots were taken, so his feet were wrapped with rags and tree bark to try to protect them.

Tate and Atwater had been there longer than him, so the condition of their health and their "clothing" was even worse. But that wouldn't stop the Raiders from trying to steal what they did have.

"Clint?" Atwater said.

"Yes, Dorence?"

"Are you really fixing the Confederate soldiers' guns?" the younger man asked.

"I am," he said. "It was the only way to keep you and Tate and some of the others alive."

"Can't you do somethin' to them?" Atwater asked.

"Like what, kid?" Tate asked.

"I don't know," Atwater said, "somethin' that would make them explode when they tried to fire them?"

"That'd be great," Tate said. "And the first time that happened, they'd kill Clint, and then you, and then me . . ."

"Can't do it, Dorence," Clint said, "but they won't be firing their guns unless we give them a reason to."

"Like tryin' to escape?"

"That's right."

"But isn't it our duty to try?"

"It's not our duty to get killed," Clint said, "or do I have that wrong, Lieutenant?"

"Not in my book, Adams," Tate said. "Our duty is to try to get out of here if we can, but to get out alive, and not feet first."

Being on patrol was tricky. You still had to stay pretty close to barracks or risk some armed guard thinking you were trying to escape. However, if Regulator met Raider and a fight ensued, the Confederate guards usually stood back and watched and, in some cases, made wagers.

Clint, Tate, and Dorence were outside their own barracks when the Raiders hit. They came in a swarm, screaming as they did to try to terrify their prey. The tactic worked with Atwater, who shrank away, but Clint and Tate both turned to meet the onslaught with their weapons.

They were outnumbered nearly four-to-one, but the Raiders were as emaciated and weak as any of the other prisoners. Clint and Tate were almost able to shrug them off. They swung their weapons, Clint's club landing solidly, the nails at the end of Tate's board tearing flesh, and yet they did their best not to kill. They were, after all, fighting their own men.

Two Confederate guards stood by with their rifles in their arms, watching the action, pointing and laughing. By the time the Raiders had had enough and retreated, dragging their wounded with them, one guard shook his head and handed the other guard some money.

"You okay?" Clint asked Tate, panting from exertion.

"Not hurt," the lieutenant said. "Damn, I wanted to try and grab one of them."

"No," Clint said, "they always manage to take their wounded with them. Where's Dorence?"

They both turned, saw Atwater rolled up into a ball on the ground.

"Dorence?" Clint said, bending over him. "You all right? Are you hurt?"

"N-No," Atwater said, uncoiling and staring at Clint, wide-eyed. "I'm not hurt. I'm just . . . a coward."

"Never mind," Clint said, helping the boy to his feet. "It doesn't matter."

Clint turned, saw the look of distaste on the face of Lieutenant Tate, but the officer kept his opinions to himself.

"Come on, kid," Clint said. "Let's get you inside. Time to get some sleep."

# FIFTEEN

Clint woke with a start, turned his head, and saw Molly staring straight ahead. She sensed he was awake and looked at him.

"You okay?" she asked.

"Yeah, I'm fine," he said, even though there was a sheen of sweat on his forehead. "I'll stay awake for a while. You get some sleep."

"Okay," she said without argument. She closed her eyes, and fell asleep immediately. He studied her profile for a few moments. He hoped that when this was all over, she'd turn out to be exactly what she claimed to be. He still wasn't able to trust her completely, which was a shame.

But did he even trust Tate? He hadn't seen the man since they were expatriated from Andersonville. After that experience they had each gone their separate ways, had not kept in touch in any way. As a matter of fact, over the years Clint had not seen any of the men he was at Camp Sumter with. This had been the first time he'd heard Dorence Atwater's name in all that time.

Atwater had been a coward, there was no doubt about

that. It shamed him, no matter how much Clint tried to convince him that every man couldn't be brave. But his cowardice had cost no one except himself, which made it easier for Clint to forgive.

Now, however, these many years later, Dorence Atwater was suddenly convinced he had to kill the man he thought was Henry Wirz? Wasn't this much, much too late to suddenly show some courage?

Clint craned his neck to study the other passengers on the train. He was still only concerned with two, the two armed men he had seen on the platform. They were paying no attention to him, but that meant they were paying no attention to Molly, which he found odd. Of course, since she was obviously with him, that might have explained why the two men were not looking at a pretty woman on the train.

The conductor walked by, nodding at Clint and giving Molly an appreciative look. There were no other young women in the car, which was far from filled. Clint decided he had to continue watching the two men until they parted ways at some point during the trip.

# SIXTEEN

They took one train north and another east before they arrived in Saint Louis and climbed aboard their private military train. It consisted of an engine, a stock car, a caboose, and a passenger car that had been specially outfitted for comfort. He knew his friend Jim West sometimes used a train like this, but this was Clint's first time to travel in such comfort.

"Real beds?" Molly said. "And a kitchen?"

"But no cook," Clint said. "We're not that lucky."

"I've seen the train Jim sometimes travels on with his partner, and they do have a cook," she said.

"That's okay," Clint said. "I don't think we'll be on this train long enough to need a cook."

They made themselves comfortable on a sofa, waiting for the train to start moving. The passenger car had a stuffed sofa and armchairs, and a table large enough to eat or strategize on, all of which were bolted to the floor so they wouldn't shift. They had met the engineer and the conductor, who were apparently armed with the proper code words, which they exchanged with Molly. If Clint had completely trusted Molly, that would have eased Clint's mind somewhat, but he was determined to remain at a heightened state of attention. At least the two men he'd been watching when they left Atlanta were out of the picture.

They were still waiting for the train to begin moving when the back door of their car opened suddenly. Clint stood, ready to draw his gun if necessary, but it was Private Collins who entered, followed by Colonel Frederick Tate. Both men were in full uniform.

"Colonel."

Molly stood as the superior officer entered the car.

"Stay outside, Collins," Tate said. "And be alert."

"Yes, sir."

Collins left, and Tate turned to face Clint and Molly.

"Congratulations on making it this far," he said. "I understand there was some problems."

"You couldn't have been gone very long after our first meeting," Clint said. "You must have heard the shots."

"I had confidence that you'd be able to handle it," Tate said. "After all, that's what you do, isn't it?"

"I don't like getting shot at," Clint said. "I don't care how often it happens,"

"I'm sorry," Tate said.

"Do you have any idea who was shooting at me?" Clint asked.

"No."

"Any idea how they knew where I'd be?"

"None."

"Do you think they knew I was meeting with you?" Clint asked.

"I don't know, Clint," Tate said. "I'm sorry, but I don't know how—"

"Who knows what I'm doing for you?" Clint asked. "Besides you and the private?"

"I know."

"No one else?"

"No," Tate said. "The private knows nothing."

"And the Secret Service?"

Tate looked at Molly.

"I only told her bosses I needed you," Tate said, "and I wanted Jim West's help in finding you. Do you mind if I sit?"

"Be our guest," Molly said.

Tate sat in one of the chairs. Clint and Molly sat back down on the sofa.

"Do you have news to share?" Clint asked.

"Some," Tate said. "Dorence Atwater is still in San Francisco."

"That's good, isn't it?" Molly asked. "With the senator in Washington?"

"The senator is not staying in Washington," Tate said. "He's going to San Francisco."

"When?" Clint asked.

"In about a week."

"Can you stop him?"

"No," Tate said. "The senator is not the kind of man you stop from doing anything he wants to do."

"Not even to save his life?" Clint asked.

"Especially not then," Tate said.

"Then he's a fool," Clint said.

"That may be, but he could well become president of the United States one day."

"He won't get my vote," Clint said.

Tate stiffened and glared at Clint, who thought for a moment that the man was going to take him to task, but then Tate seemed to relax.

"Nevertheless," Tate said, "we can't let him be killed."

"Come on, sir," Clint said. "This is Dorence Atwater we're talking about, remember? Do you think he's changed after all these years?"

"I think," Tate said, "even a devout coward may change if given one last chance to redeem himself."

"And that's what you think this is?" Clint asked. "An attempt at redemption?"

"What else could it be?" Tate asked. "Vengeance? It's not like Atwater had many friends in Andersonville, if I remember correctly. His cowardice kept him from making any friends."

"That seems cruel," Molly said.

Tate looked at her as if noticing for the first time she was there.

"I'm sorry, if you find that cruel, Molly," he said. "I can't help that. None of the men suffering in Andersonville appreciated Atwater's cowardice."

"And none of them were cowards?"

"None of them seemed to revel in it," Tate said.

"That's unfair," Clint said.

"I don't agree," Tate said, "but that's neither here nor there. It's past. We have to deal with the future."

"And Senator Harlan is the future?" Clint asked. "Of this country?"

"He may very well be."

"I don't like politics much, sir," Clint said.

"Nobody's asking you to become involved in politics," Tate said. "You're just being asked to keep the senator alive when he goes to San Francisco."

"How do you expect me to do that?"

"That's your business," Tate said. "Meet with Atwater, dissuade him, do what you have to do. No questions will be asked."

Clint leaned forward. Molly could feel the tension in his body.

"Are you telling me that no questions will be asked if I decide to kill Atwater?"

"I'm not condoning murder," Tate said. "I'm just telling

you, your methods are your own, and no, they will not be questioned."

Tate stood up.

"Watch each other's backs," Tate said. "Molly." He touched his hat, and left.

Clint sat back.

"He wants you to kill Atwater."

"He wanted to kill him when we were in Andersonville," Clint said.

"And you wouldn't let him?"

"Oh, he never really tried, but I could tell in the way he looked at Dorence," Clint said. "He wanted him gone."

"And you kept Atwater alive?" she asked.

"I suppose."

"Then you should be able to talk him out of this madness," she said.

"I don't know," Clint said. "If what Tate says is true and Atwater sees this at his last chance at redemption . . . that will be hard to talk him out of."

"You wouldn't kill him, would you?"

"Not to save a politician's life," Clint said.

# SEVENTEEN

The ride from Saint Louis to San Francisco was made in the lap of luxury, but the meeting with Tate had cast a veil over it.

The conductor came in at one point and said, "We're a half an hour out, sir."

"Thanks," Clint said.

"You've been quiet most of the way," Molly said.

"Thinking."

"About Atwater?"

"Atwater, Tate," Clint said, "and the senator. Have you heard of him before?"

"No," she said. "I don't really pay attention to politics. I just do my job."

"I'm the same," he said. "I know the names of prominent politicians, but I'd never heard of Harlan until this."

"What does that mean to you?"

"It makes me wonder," Clint said, "how the man got so important."

"What do you intend to do?"

"I suppose," Clint said, "I'll do what I did the whole time I was in Andersonville."

"What's that?"

"Keep Dorence Atwater alive."

When the train pulled into the station in San Francisco, it attracted some attention. Clint wasn't happy about it, but what could he do? Curious onlookers watched as he walked Eclipse out of the stock car.

"What's first?" Molly asked.

"I want to send some telegrams," he said. "I have friends who might be able to help me with several questions."

"Where are we going to stay?"

"I have a place in mind," he said. "Not as luxurious as the train, but we want to keep a low profile."

Clint had been to San Francisco many times, more often than not staying in one of the big gambling palaces in or near Portsmouth Square. But not this time.

"The Barbary Coast?" Molly asked.

"Nobody will look for us here."

Molly glanced around as they walked down the street.

"Everybody's looking at us," she said.

"They're looking at you," he said. "A pretty woman is a valuable commodity on the Coast."

"Now you tell me."

"Once we get a room, we'll do something about that," he said.

"Like what?" she asked. "Break my nose?"

"No, nothing that drastic," he promised, "but we can do something to make sure you're not shanghaied."

"Shanghaied?" she asked. "I wasn't even thinking about that. Thanks a lot."

"Stop worrying."

They were approaching the hotel Clint had chosen for their stay.

Clint had been to the Bucket of Blood before when he didn't want anyone to know he was in San Francisco. He didn't know who owned the hotel, and the same clerk was never behind the desk when he went there. But there were never any questions asked, even when he showed up with a woman.

He registered for both of them under a phony name and got two rooms.

"Why two rooms?" she asked as they went up the stairs. "I mean, after Atlanta—"

"I'm just playing it safe," Clint said. "We'll sleep in one room one night, and the other room the next night."

"Oh, I see."

Upstairs he tossed his saddlebags on the bed. He had gotten Eclipse settled in a stable near the railroad station. He probably wasn't going to need the horse while in San Francisco, and normally would not have brought him along, but if he had left the horse in Atlanta, he would have had to go back there for him. This way, when he was done in San Francisco, he had the option of leaving by train, or on horse-back.

"What now?" she asked.

"Now," he said, "we find Dorence Atwater."

# EIGHTEEN

Dorence Atwater worked for a small San Francisco newspaper called *The Reporter.* The office was on Market Street, an area Clint knew well. The building was a three-story stone structure, pitted from years of weather. The paper had offices on the second floor. The first and third floors were empty.

"This is where the newspaper is?" Molly asked, staring up at the building.

"Maybe they'll move sometime, but for now this is it," he said.

"It looks abandoned."

They went inside and up a musty stairway to the second floor. There, suddenly, the image of an abandoned building disappeared. People were rushing around, usually with pieces of paper in their hands. One young girl was hurrying by when Clint reached out to stop her.

"I'm looking for Dorence Atwater," he said.

"Down that hall, to the left."

"His office?"

"No," she said as if he was crazy. "His desk."

"Thanks."

She continued on. Clint and Molly went down the hall. When Clint saw Atwater, he recognized him immediately. He had changed, filled out, and his hair—though still blond—was sparse, but Clint knew it was him.

"Dorence?"

"I'm a little busy—" Atwater started, but when he looked up and saw Clint, he stopped short, narrowed his eyes, then smiled.

"Clint Adams?"

"That's right."

"Well, sonofagun," Atwater said, standing. He was still rail thin, as if he'd never been able to put back the weight he'd lost in Andersonville. "How the hell are you?"

The two men shook hands.

"And who's this?" Atwater asked.

"Meet Molly O'Henry," Clint said.

"Miss O'Henry."

"Mr. Atwater," she said. "Nice to meet you."

"What brings you here?" he asked Clint.

"We came to take you out for a drink," Clint said. "Or how about lunch?"

"How about both?" Atwater said. He grabbed his jacket from the back of his chair. "Let's go."

"Do you have to clear it with someone?" Clint asked.

"Believe me," Atwater said, "nobody cares."

He hurried down the hall and descended the stairs. Clint and Molly followed.

# NINETEEN

Atwater led them to a watering hole just a couple of blocks from the newspaper office. Inside, the bartender greeted him by name. He led them to a table in the back that seemed to be a regular spot for him.

The bartender brought a bottle of whiskey over, then looked at Clint and Molly.

"Beer," Clint said.

"The same," Molly said.

"Food?" Clint asked Atwater.

"This is my lunch," Atwater said, pouring himself a glass of whiskey.

"I'm hungry," Molly said.

"What have you got in the way of food?" Clint asked.

"This ain't a restaurant," the man said. "We got sandwiches—"

"Bring them some of your mother's beef stew, Al," Atwater said. "They're friends of mine."

The bartender, a big, beefy, tough-looking man, suddenly smiled and looked several years younger, and not so tough.

"Comin' up!" he said.

He brought the beers over first, and then they talked while they waited for the food. Atwater had downed three drinks very quickly, and was sipping at a fourth.

"Okay," he said, "now I feel human. How did you find me, Clint? And more importantly, why?"

"I think you know why, Dorence."

Atwater looked at Molly.

"Has he told you where we met?"

"He has."

"And that he kept me alive?"

"Yes."

Atwater looked at Clint.

"It's him, Clint," he said. "It's Wirz."

He finished his fourth drink, poured another. The bartender returned with two steaming bowls of beef stew, and another bowl filled with pieces of thick bread.

"My sainted mother's recipe," he said. "Enjoy."

"Thank you," Clint said.

The bartender withdrew.

"Taste it," Atwater said to Molly. "It's great."

Molly took a forkful, raised her eyebrows.

"That's wonderful."

Clint tasted it, found it the same. Atwater poured himself another drink.

"It's him," Atwater said over the rim of his glass. His eyes were glazed. "It's Wirz, damn it."

"Wirz is dead," Clint said. "Executed. Hanged in front of witnesses."

"I know, I know," Atwater said. "You think I don't know that? But I have seen that man's face every night in my dreams since Andersonville. And I'm telling you, Senator Harlan Winston is Henry Wirz."

"Let's suppose you're right," Clint said. "Suppose Wirz wasn't executed, for some reason. How could he possibly become a senator? He wasn't even born in this country."

"Maybe Henry Wirz wasn't," Atwater said, "but Harlan Winston was supposedly born in Georgia."

"Wirz had a thick accent."

"What better way to cover up a foreign accent than with a Southern one?" Atwater asked. "A syrupy Southern accent."

And don't you see the irony of Winston claiming to have been born in Georgia?"

"Okay," Clint said, "okay. So what do you plan to do?"

"I plan to kill him."

"You're going to assassinate a United States senator," Clint asked.

"I have to," Atwater said.

"Why?" Clint asked. "Because you were a coward in Andersonville."

Atwater looked at Molly quickly.

"She's heard everything," Clint said. "From me. From Tate."

"Lieutenant Tate?"

"Colonel, now," Clint said.

"Colonel," Atwater said, nodding. "That figures."

"Dorence," Clint said, "why don't you just expose Winston?"

"That's not enough," Atwater said. "Not nearly enough for what he did."

"But for Wirz to escape execution, change his name, and become a senator . . . he had to have a lot of help," Clint said. "Who, in our government, would help the commandant of Camp Sumter, and why?"

"I don't know who and why," Atwater said. "That's not important to me. I saw him, here in San Francisco, and I knew it was him. And he's coming back. And when he does, I'll be ready."

"So suddenly, you're a killer?" Clint asked. "How are you going to do it? With a rifle? You can fire a rifle now?"

"All I have to do is get close enough," Atwater said. "I'll

kill him with my bare hands if I have to." Suddenly, Atwater's left hand shot out and grabbed Clint's arm. In his right he still held his whiskey glass.

"You can help me!" he said urgently. "You know what he did. You were there!"

"I was there," Clint said. "I know what Henry Wirz did. But this . . . this can't be him, Dorence."

"What if I can prove it to you?" Atwater asked. "What if I can prove that Harlan Winston is Henry Wirz? Will you help me then?"

Clint studied Atwater for a few moments, then looked at Atwater.

"I think I'll have a glass of whiskey," he said.

# TWENTY

By the end of "lunch" Atwater was too drunk to go back to work. Clint managed to get his address from him, and he and Molly took him home. He had a small room on the second floor of another run-down building that was only blocks from his office.

They dropped him onto his bed, then Clint wrote him a note, saying they'd come back and see him the next day.

"Stay sober until you see us," he wrote, and left the note next to the bed.

Then they left.

On the street Molly said, "You wouldn't do it, would you?"

"Do what?"

"Actually help him kill Winston."

"I wouldn't help him kill Senator Harlan Winston," Clint said.

"But would you help him kill Henry Wirz?"

"You want an honest answer?"

"I'd appreciate it."

Clint hesitated, then said, "I don't know. That's my

honest answer. If he proves to me that Henry Wirz is alive . . . I just don't know."

Before leaving the train station Clint had sent out a couple of telegrams. The first was to Rick Hartman, his friend and source of much information, back in Labyrinth, Texas. The second was to his friend Talbot Roper, in Denver. Roper was the best private detective Clint knew. He asked them both the same question: What did they know about Senator Harlan Winston?

He told both men he'd be at the Bucket of Blood Hotel, and gave them the name he'd be registered under. He knew he was taking a chance allowing the key operator to know this information, but he felt it was worth the risk.

When he and Molly returned to the hotel, he checked with the clerk to see if any telegrams had come in for him.

"No, sir, nothin' yet," the man said.

"Let me know as soon as something comes in," Clint said, handing the man a dollar.

"Yes, sir!"

They went up to one of the rooms, the one Clint's saddlebags were in. He intended to spend the night in the other room, though. He immediately went to the window and looked out.

"You think someone's going to find us?" she asked.

"Somebody tried to kill me after my meeting with Tate, and somebody was in your house," Clint said. "It's not such a stretch to think they'd find us here."

"I guess not. Who do you suppose they were?"

"I don't know," Clint said.

"What if Winston is Wirz?" She asked. "Could be he sent some men after you?"

"How would he know about me? And why me?" Clint asked. "Why not send someone after Atwater? He's the one causing trouble."

"And how would he know about him?"

"These may all be questions we'll never know the answers to, Molly," Clint said. "The important thing is to stay alive."

"I thought the important thing was to keep the senator alive."

"That, too."

"Back on the train," Molly said, "Colonel Tate said he was the only one who knew you were coming to see Atwater."

"That's right."

"Do you think he's the only one who knows about Atwater's claim?"

"I don't see how," Clint said. "He has to report to someone."

"Does he?"

Clint rubbed his jaw.

"How would Atwater have gotten to Tate without having to go through anyone else?" he wondered.

"Is that another one of those questions?" she asked.

"Maybe not," Clint said. "That's a question we can put directly to Dorence and find out the answer to."

"You don't trust Tate, do you?"

"No."

"But I thought he was your friend."

"We were prisoners together," Clint said. "You could even say we . . . formed a bond while in Andersonville. But I don't think you can ever say we were friends."

"So you never trusted him?"

"I trusted Lieutenant Tate," Clint said. "I don't know or trust Colonel Tate."

"Do you trust me?"

"Not completely."

"Do you trust anyone completely?"

He thought a moment, then said, "About half a dozen people."

"Who are they?"

"Bat Masterson, Wyatt Earp, Luke Short, a detective named Talbot Roper, a man I know in Texas named Rick Hartman . . ."

"That's five," she said, "and all men. No women?"

"Jim West," he finished. "Women? I'm sure there have been women I trusted . . ."

"But you don't want to name names?"

"You women," he said, "you're so much more complicated than we are."

"Is that supposed to be a compliment?"

"It's just an observation," he said.

She folded her arms and regarded him from across the room. When he said nothing more on the subject, she gave up.

"What do we do now?"

"Atwater has to sober up before we get anything else out of him," Clint said. "And then we have to keep him sober until we get what we want."

"He's a drunk," she said. "It's hard to keep a drunk sober."

"I know it," he said.

"What about the senator?"

"What about him?"

"Do we know when he's coming to San Francisco?"

"In a week, I think," Clint said. "Tate didn't give me a date. I guess he didn't think it was important to what I had to do."

"Which is?"

"Stop Atwater."

She shrugged.

"I suppose you can do that without knowing his schedule," she said.

"But it would help," he said, nodding. "I should have gotten that from Tate."

"Well," she said, "we can get it from Atwater."

"I'll bet any newspaperman in this city would know," Clint said.

"Do you know any other newspapermen in San Francisco?" she asked.

"I think I might . . ."

# TWENTY-ONE

He didn't know a newspaperman, but he knew somebody who knew one. Duke Farrell ran a hotel just off Portsmouth Square that Clint owned a small piece of. The next morning Duke gave Clint the name of a newsman on the *San Francisco Examiner.*

The *Examiner*'s office was on Stevenson Street, in a much better area than *The Reporter*'s. They still had to walk up a couple of flights of stairs, though, and then suddenly the two offices looked alike, with people rushing about. Clint stopped a young man and asked for Larry Gates.

"Down the hall and to the right."

"His desk?"

The boy looked at Clint like he was mad and said, "His office!"

Clint shrugged, and he and Molly walked down the hall to Larry Gates's office.

"Larry Gates?" Clint asked as they entered.

The man who looked up from his desk was in his sixties, with white hair that hung down to his shoulders and a pair of wire-framed glasses on the tip of his nose.

"Can I help you?"

"My name's Clint Adams," Clint said. "This is Molly O'Henry."

"You're kidding," the man said.

"About what?" Clint asked.

"Clint Adams?" he asked. "The Gunsmith? Just walks into my office?"

"Looks like it."

Gates stood up and put his hand out. Clint took it. The older man then nodded to Molly, but most of his attention was fixed on Clint.

"You willin' to do an interview?" Gates asked him.

"That's not why I'm here, Mr. Gates."

"Just call me Larry," Gates said. "Everybody does. So, why are you here, then?"

"I have some questions I need answered, and I thought a newspaperman could answer them. I got your name from Duke Farrell."

"Duke? You friends with Duke? Why didn't you say so?" Gates asked. "Come on, let's go get a drink and we can talk."

"The last time I went for a drink with a newspaperman, he tried to drink me under the table and I had to put him to bed."

"I'm not a drunk, Mr. Adams," Gates said. "I'm a beer and a sandwich man. That appeal to you?" He looked at Clint, and then Molly.

"I could eat," she said.

"Good," Gates said. "Follow me."

He took them to a small restaurant a few blocks from the newspaper. It was busy, and as they walked to a table, Gates was greeted by half the people in the place.

"This is a place where newspaper people come to eat

and drink and rub elbows with each other," he explained to Clint and Molly.

It was a busy place, but there was an empty table waiting for Gates.

"Pays to have seniority," he said. "I've been working on newspapers in this town for over forty years. I even worked with Mark Twain when he wrote for the *Territorial Enterprise*."

"I know Twain," Clint said. "He's a friend of mine."

"Is that a fact?" Gates said. "You do get around, don't ya?"

"I have some friends."

"I'll bet."

A waiter came over and Gates ordered three beers and three sandwiches.

"You'll like 'em, I guarantee," Gates said. "Now, what brought you to me today? You said you had some questions?"

"About Senator Harlan Winston."

Gates frowned.

"He's comin' to San Francisco in about a week," Gates said.

"Do you know exactly when?" Clint asked.

"Not offhand, but I can check when I go back to my office."

"What do you know about the senator?"

"Not much," Gates said. "He seemed to come on the scene pretty late, but he's now in his second term, and there's some talk of him running for president at some point."

"How old is he?" Clint asked.

"I think he's in his sixties," Gates said. "About my age. Why the questions about the senator?" He leaned forward. "Is there a story in this for me?"

"There might be," Clint said, "but I can't discuss it now."

Gates sat back.

"Why's the Gunsmith interested in politics?" he asked. "And where does this lovely young lady come in?"

"I can't say," Clint answered.

The waiter came over with three beers and three roast beef sandwiches on soft bread. Gates ignored his. Molly bit into hers and nodded her head. So far the food she'd had in San Francisco had been pretty good.

"You don't know anything about Winston's past before he became a senator?"

"He was born in Georgia, served in some office there before going to Washington," Gates said. "There was a statement released when he first ran for office but there wasn't much on it. He's pretty much a mystery man."

"And Washington, and the press, accept that?"

Gates shrugged.

"He hasn't done any harm since he's been in office," Gates said.

"Has he done any good?" Molly asked.

Gates looked at her and grinned.

"You know, that's a very good question."

# TWENTY-TWO

They ate their lunch and then accompanied Gates back to the offices of the *Examiner*. When they got there, Gates went into his file cabinet to see what he could find on Senator Winston.

"Nope, not much," Gates said. "Even the statements his people released are sketchy."

"How does a man get into public office and keep his past a secret?" Clint asked.

Gates closed his file cabinet drawer and turned to face Clint.

"Why are you so interested in his past?" he asked. "What do you think is there?"

"I can't say right now," Clint answered.

"You can't say much," Gates said. "You're bein' as secretive as the senator."

Clint didn't respond.

"What will I find out about you from Duke?" Gates asked.

"Not much, but go ahead and ask," Clint said.

"I think I will." Gates looked at Molly. "And who do I ask about you, young lady?"

"Ask Clint," she suggested.

"Won't be much forthcoming from there, I'm afraid," Gates said.

"Then I guess you'll just have to wait," Clint said.

"If there's a story, will you give it to me?" Gates asked.

"If there's a story that needs to be told," Clint said, "I'll give it to you."

"And an interview."

"I don't do interviews, Mr. Gates."

"I know," Gates said. "That's why gettin' one would be so exciting."

"I'm sorry—"

"Well, maybe if I can come up with somethin' for you, you'll reconsider."

"Maybe," Clint said. "No promises."

"I'm not askin' for promises," Gates said. "Just say there's a chance."

"Okay, Larry," Clint said, "there's a chance . . ."


"But not much of one," Clint said when he and Molly got outside.

"Why don't you like interviews?" she asked.

"Because newspaper people tend to write whatever they want."

"Newspaper people?"

He nodded.

"Men or women, it doesn't really matter much."

"So what do we do now?" she asked.

"Head back to the hotel, see if I got any telegrams," Clint said.

After they'd walked awhile, Molly asked, "Will you really give Gates the story—if there is a story?"

"I don't know," Clint said. "He wasn't very helpful, was he?"

"Maybe he'll come up with something, though," she said.

"Maybe he will," Clint said. "I guess I'll decide if and when that happens."

As soon as they walked in the hotel door, the clerk started waving at Clint.

"You got two telegrams, Mr. Adams," he said, handing them over.

"Thanks."

"I knocked on your door," the clerk went on. "Tried to get them to you earlier, but you wasn't there."

"I appreciate it," Clint said, and handed the clerk a dollar, making him very happy.

"What do they say?" Molly asked.

"Come on," he said, "we'll read them upstairs."

They had spent the night in Room 6, so when they went up, Clint let them into Room 7. Once inside, he opened the telegrams and read them.

"You look disappointed," she said.

"These are two of the men I trust the most to get me information," he said, speaking of Rick Hartman and Talbot Roper.

"And?"

"They both came up with the same thing as Gates," he said. "Which is to say, not much. Senator Harlan Winston is still a mystery man."

"I guess we should have asked some questions about him while we were still in Georgia," she said.

"And I would have," Clint said, "if Colonel Tate had told me he was from Georgia. And if Tate hadn't been in such an all-fired hurry to get me out here to San Francisco."

# TWENTY-THREE

Clint had depended on either Rick or Roper to get him some information. He was disappointed. That only left Dorence Atwater to get information from.

He and Molly went back to the offices of *The Reporter* and found Atwater sitting at his desk. Clint was surprised that the man did not look like he had been drinking the day before.

"Good afternoon, you two," Atwater said. "Sorry about yesterday. Guess I drank a little too much at lunch. Thanks for getting me home."

"That's okay," Clint said. "No harm. Mind if we sit?"

"Are we going to talk about . . . the same things as yesterday?" Atwater asked.

"I'd like to—"

"Well, we can't do that here then," Atwater said, standing. "If I get fired from this job, I won't get another one with a newspaper. This is my last job in journalism."

He rushed past them to the stairway and they had to hurry to catch up to him by the time they got to the main floor.

"Where are we going?" Clint asked.

"Dinner," Atwater said.

"Look, Dorence—"

"Not the same kind of dinner as yesterday," Atwater promised, "although that was lunch, not dinner. No, I'm not going to drink myself into a coma today, Clint. I'm taking us someplace where we can talk. I mean, really talk."

"Okay," Clint said, looking at Molly. "Lead the way."

It seemed to Clint he was spending all of his time in restaurants, either with Atwater or Gates. Was that all that the newspapermen in San Francisco did—eat and drink?

Atwater took them to a restaurant that was surprisingly nicer than the one they'd gone to the day before. At the door he found out why.

"Dinner's on you, right?" Atwater asked. "I haven't been able to afford this place in a long time."

"It's on me," Clint said.

They went inside.

Atwater ate as if he hadn't eaten in months.

"I would have bought you something to eat yesterday," Clint pointed out.

"Yesterday I needed whiskey," Atwater said. "Today I need food."

"Do you ever need both on the same day?" Molly asked. "Or neither?"

"Sure," Atwater said, "but lately I've had more days when I need food."

"Why?" Molly asked.

"Because I have to keep my strength up," he said. "When the time comes, I have to be strong enough to do what must be done."

"And what is that?" Molly asked. "What must be done?"

"I have to kill Henry Wirz," Atwater said. "See, if I had

been able to keep up my strength in Andersonville, I might have been able to do it then."

"You never would have been able to do it then, Dorence," Clint said.

Around a huge mouthful of food Atwater asked, "Why not?"

"Because no amount of food or water would have given you courage," Clint said. "And no amount of food or whiskey will give you courage this time."

Atwater stopped chewing. Suddenly, he leaned forward and spit the food back into the plate, then pushed the plate away.

"I need whiskey," he said.

"Later," Clint said. "We need to talk."

"About what?"

"Senator Winston."

"You mean Henry Wirz."

"I mean Harlan Winston," Clint said. "Have you done any research into his background?"

"It's enough for me that he claims to be from Georgia," Atwater said. "Don't you see. Henry Wirz died in Georgia, and Harlan Winston was born. Don't you see, Clint?"

"No, I don't see, Dorence," Clint said. "I need more proof."

"You'll have all the proof you need," Atwater said. "All you have to do is wait here until he arrives. When you see him, you'll know him, Clint."

# TWENTY-FOUR

They went from the restaurant to a nearby saloon and stood at the bar. Apparently, it had gone from being a food day to a whiskey day for Dorence Atwater.

While Atwater drank, Molly asked Clint, "Are we just going to let him get drunk again?"

"Well," Clint said, "he made a good point."

"What point?"

"When I see Harlan Winston," he said, "I'll know if he's Henry Wirz."

"And then what?" she asked. "He'll still be a U.S. senator."

"If Winston is Wirz," Clint said, "then somebody helped him escape execution and change his name. And somebody helped him become a senator. I'd like to know who, and why. Wouldn't you?"

"I never heard of Henry Wirz until all of this," she said. "I really don't care if Wirz is Winston, or if Winston is Wirz. I'm just trying to do my job."

"That's because you weren't there," Clint said. "And you're too young to remember."

"So what are you going to do?"

They looked at Atwater, who was tossing back another whiskey.

"I can't believe he'd be able to kill anyone, Wirz or otherwise," Clint said.

"So you don't think he's a danger to the senator?" Molly said.

"Not in this condition," Clint said.

"Drunk?"

"No," Clint said, "I'm pretty sure he's still a coward, and no amount of whiskey is going to change that."

"Maybe not."

"Would you like a drink?" he asked

"Maybe a small one."

In a corner of the saloon three men sat and watched as Atwater drank.

"You think he's tol' them about us?" Angus Edwards asked.

"I don't think the newspaperman has been in shape to tell them much of anything," Ted Bellows said.

"That's Clint Adams, though," Jake Fester said. "He was at Camp Sumter with us."

"That may be," Bellows said, "but he was a Regulator and we was Raiders. He never did see us."

"But he busted us up," Edwards said.

"Yeah, but we wasn't among the ones who got tried and convicted, was we?" Bellows asked. "No, they was happy with the few they caught."

"And with Parker," Fester reminded them. "Don't forget Parker."

"How could I forget Frank Parker?" Bellows said. "After all, he was our leader, right?"

"So what're we gonna do now?" Fester asked. "If Adams keeps at Atwater, he'll talk eventually."

"I don't think so," Bellows said. "Atwater ain't no different here than he was at Camp Sumter. He's a coward. He'd be too afraid to tell Adams that he joined up with us."

"I thought we joined up with him because he recognized Wirz," Fester said.

"Never mind who joined who," Bellows said. "Atwater recognized Wirz, that's all we need to know. It don't matter if we was Raiders or Regulators. We all hated the Johnny Rebs, and we hated Wirz more than all the others."

"I can't wait to kill 'im," Edwards said.

"Let's keep an eye on Atwater," Bellows said, "and keep an eye on Adams and the girl. It's less than a week 'til the senator gets here. By that time maybe Adams will join up with us. After all, he hated Henry Wirz just as much as we did."

"He made a deal with Wirz, remember?" Edwards asked. "Got extra rations."

"For him and his Regulators," Bellows said. "It ain't like he was a traitor or nothin'."

Fester's face was all scrunched up as he tried to think it out.

"How do we keep an eye on all of them at the same time?" he finally asked, giving up on trying to figure it out.

"We separate, you idiot," Bellows said. "We split up."

# TWENTY-FIVE

Clint and Molly dropped Dorence Atwater into his bed again.

"I hope we don't have to do this every night," she said.

"We won't," Clint said, "because we won't be seeing him every night."

As they walked back down the stairs, Molly said, "I wonder how he keeps from being fired."

"Who knows?" Clint asked. "Maybe he was a decent newspaperman before he got obsessed with Senator Harlan Winston being Henry Wirz."

"That's not the way it sounded to me," she said, "him saying this was his last job. Sounds like he's pretty much been messing up his whole life."

"Or at least," Clint said, "since he got out of Andersonville."

"What about the rest of you?" she asked.

"What about us?"

"Why haven't you messed up your life?"

"Who says I haven't?" he asked.

"What do you mean?"

"I came out of Andersonville angry," he said. "I started looking for a fight wherever I went. Much of my reputation was gained in the few years after the war. Even Lincoln's death fueled my anger."

"No," she said, "everything I've heard from Jim West, and what I've seen since I met you, tells me you haven't messed up your life."

"Well," Clint said, "many others have."

"What about Tate?"

"I can't speak for Tate," Clint said, "but he is a colonel."

They were on the street now, walking side by side. She put her hand on his arm to stop him.

"You've been trying to check up on Senator Winston," she said.

"Yeah. So?"

"Why not check up on the colonel?"

He frowned at her, but the frown was meant for himself.

"I should have thought of that," he said. "It's a good idea."

"So? More telegrams?"

He nodded.

"More telegrams."

# TWENTY-SIX

They went to the same telegraph office as before and Clint sent two telegrams. The clerk was instructed to send any replies to the Bucket of Blood.

"To the same two people?" she asked afterward.

"Yes."

"I thought you were disappointed in them."

"I was disappointed in what they found out," he said. "Actually, there is a third telegram I wish I could send."

"To who?"

"Jim West."

"Maybe I can help there," she said, turning around. "Let's go back inside."

"You know were he is?"

"I know a few telegraph drops around the country," she said. "All we have to do is send the same telegram to each one. At some point, he'll pick one up."

"All right," he said. "Let's do it, then."

They went back to their hotel, nodded to the clerk on the way in. He looked away.

"Stop," Clint said at the top of the stairs.

"What is it?"

"Something's wrong."

"Why?"

"The clerk didn't look at us," Clint said. "In fact, he looked away."

"He's always looking for an extra dollar."

"That's right."

"Somebody's in our room?"

"Somebody's in one of our rooms," he said.

"Do you think it has anything to do with the men following us?"

"You saw them?"

"Oh, yeah," she said. "They're not very good."

"We can deal with them later," he said. "This one is in our room, which makes him more of a concern."

"Could be the same one who was in my house," she commented.

"Let's find out."

They started down the hall. Molly drew her gun. Clint left his in his holster, but he was ready to produce it if the need arose.

"Which room?" she asked.

Rooms 6 and 7 were across from each other. He looked at both doors in turn.

"Both," he said. "You take six, I'll take seven. On my mark."

She stood by the door of Room 6. He drew his gun and stood by the door of Room 7. They both listened, then shook their heads. She watched him, and when he nodded, they each opened the door.

The rooms were empty, but had obviously been gone through. The contents of Clint's saddlebags were on the bed and the floor. Extra shirt, extra gun, a book he was reading.

"This reminds me," she said.

"What?"

"We have to do some shopping," she said. "We've been walking around in the same clothes for days."

# TWENTY-SEVEN

Before they went shopping for clothes, Clint decided they should have a talk with the clerk. When they went back downstairs, he wasn't behind the desk.

"Look behind the desk," Clint said. "I'll check outside."

Clint went outside and looked both ways. The men following them were across the street, trying to look inconspicuous. He decided it couldn't have been them in the rooms. They had been following him and Molly most of the day.

When he went back inside, she was coming out from the curtained doorway behind the desk.

"There's an office back there. Nobody in it."

"So he just walked away from his job?" Clint said.

"Away from you, probably," she said. "If he knows who you are . . ."

"We signed in under a phony name," he said.

"Maybe somebody told him. If so, he'd be afraid you were going to kill him."

"Then why let somebody into the rooms?"

"Maybe," she said, "somebody gave him more than a dollar."

"Maybe."

"Can we go shopping?"

"It's late," he said. "Stores will be closed."

"It's not dark yet."

"It will be soon."

"So what do we do?" she asked. "Just stay in one of our rooms?"

"No," he said.

He walked behind the desk, looked at the pegs the room keys were hanging on. Only theirs and two others were missing. The hotel was practically empty.

He collected all the rest of the keys, then turned and looked at Molly.

"We have our pick," he said. "One room for each of us."

"Separate rooms?"

He nodded.

"We need to keep alert," he said. "In a room together that would be . . . hard."

"What about the two outside?" she asked.

"They're just following us," he said. "Tomorrow we'll let them watch us shop."

"And then what?"

"Then we'll surprise them and ask some questions."

"Okay, so how do we choose a room?"

He smiled, held his hand out with a bunch of keys in his palm.

"Pick one."

Outside, Fester and Edwards watched impatiently.

"What's goin' on?" Edwards asked. "Why'd he come back out, and then go back in?"

"Let's find out."

They crossed the street, approached the hotel carefully. When they peered inside, they saw that the lobby was empty. There was no one behind the desk.

They entered and walked to the desk.

"Look," Edwards said.

"What?"

"No keys."

"So they took all the keys, so what? What's that mean?" Bellows asked.

"We better tell Bellows," Edwards said. "Maybe he can figure out what it means."

"He said to watch them."

"Okay," Edwards said, "you keep watching the hotel, I'll go and talk to Bellows."

"Why do I have to stay?"

"One of us has to," Edwards said. "I'll be back. Don't worry."

They went back outside.

"Go back across the street," Edwards said. "I'll be back soon."

"You better be."

"Don't worry."

"Yeah," Fester said. "What if they see me?"

"Don't let 'em," Edwards said.

# TWENTY-EIGHT

Clint chose a room that did not look out on the street. That way the men who were following him couldn't see his light. But he went into a room across the hall so he could look out a front window. It took him a moment, but he located a doorway with the lighted tip of a cigarette in it. It was almost dark, but he thought he could see one man there. Maybe the other one went for instructions. If he'd known that was going to happen, he would have followed him.

He went back across the hall to his room and found Molly lying on the bed with her boots off.

"I thought we said separate rooms," he said.

"Yeah, I thought about that," she said. "But if they don't know what room we're in, what does it matter?"

"They can see the light in the window, or under the door."

"That's why I lit the lamps in half a dozen rooms. They'd have to go through all of them to get to us."

"Unless they pick this one first."

"Damn you," she said. "I never thought of that."

"But I don't think they will."

"Why not?"

"One of them is gone," he said. "Probably went to report to whoever sent them."

"Damn," she said again, "we could have followed him, found out who that is."

"We'll do that tomorrow," he said.

"What about Atwater?" she asked. "Should we talk to him again?"

"I think when we talk to him," Clint said, "that's when he starts to drink."

"So are we just going to stay around here until the senator shows up?"

"Tomorrow we'll see what information our telegrams bring."

"But even if we find out Tate is acting alone, on his own authority, we can't leave Atwater here to kill the senator."

"I don't think he will," Clint said. "I don't think he'd be able to. He hasn't changed that much."

She sat up on the bed and asked, "What if he has help?"

"Who?"

"I don't know," she said. "Maybe those two that were following us all day. Maybe they're also from Andersonville. Maybe Atwater found somebody who feels the same way he does."

"Well," he said, "there were almost forty-five thousand prisoners in Andersonville over the years."

"Jesus," she said. "That many? And how many of them died there?"

"About twelve thousand."

"I had no idea."

"But you've got a pretty good idea now," he said. "If Atwater knew he'd never have the nerve to kill the senator, he'd get help."

"All he'd have to do is find somebody else from Andersonville who hated Wirz."

"And convince them that Winston is Wirz."

She lay back down on the bed, her hands folded over her stomach.

"Not much we can do about it tonight," she said. "What do we do about the missing clerk? Who's going to accept our telegrams?"

"The owner's got to realize his clerk is gone and replace him," Clint said. "I mean, at some point."

"That leaves the question of what we do tonight," she said. "Sleep in separate rooms?"

"Or sleep at all?" he asked.

She was wearing the same dress she'd worn the day before, although they had both given their clothes a less-than-half-decent wash the night before, using the pitcher and basin in the room. They really did need to buy some new clothes.

She pulled the dress up to her waist, revealing her nude patch.

"Like I said in Atlanta," she said, "we could keep each other awake."

Her Colt Paterson was on the table next to the bed. He hadn't asked her where she carried it when they were on the street.

He grabbed the wooden chair in the room, stuck the back of it under the doorknob, then removed his gun belt and hung it on the bed post.

"Does this mean I've convinced you?" she asked.

"No," he said, sliding his hand down into her tangled patch, but this does . . ."

# TWENTY-NINE

Bellows and Atwater were sitting at a table in a small saloon they used to meet.

"You're gettin' drunk too much," Bellows said.

"What do you care?"

"I care because drunk, you might tell Clint Adams somethin' you're not supposed to."

"I'm not going to tell him anything I don't want to tell him," Atwater said.

"I hope not," Bellows said. "You could end up blowin' our whole plan."

"*Our* plan?" the newspaperman asked.

"Okay, your plan," Bellows said. "Whatever. I just don't want you ruinin' it."

"Don't you worry," Atwater said, "we're going to kill Henry Wirz."

"As soon as you convince me this Senator Winston is Wirz," Bellows added.

"You'll see," Atwater said. "You'll see for yourselves. You'll know him when you see him."

They were having another drink when Edwards entered

the saloon. For Bellows it was his second beer. As far as Atwater was concerned, they had both lost count.

"What the hell are you doing here?" Bellows demanded.

"Don't worry," Edwards said. "Fester is watching them.
Adams and the girl are at their hotel."

"Where?" Atwater asked.

"The Bucket of Blood."

"Where is that?" the newspaperman asked.

"The Barbary Coast," Edwards said.

"What are they doing there?"

"Hidin' out," Bellows said. He looked at Edwards. "Why
are you here?"

"The hotel lobby is empty," Edwards said. "There's no
clerk, and there are no room keys."

"Is the hotel full?" Atwater asked.

"No," Edwards said. "We checked earlier. Adams and
the girl have their own rooms. Other than them, there are
only two other rooms occupied."

Atwater started to laugh.

"What's so funny?" Bellow demanded.

"They spotted you."

"What makes you say that?"

"They've taken all the keys so you won't know what
room they're in."

"And the clerk?" Edwards asked. "Did they kill him?"

"No," Atwater said. "He probably did something stupid
and ran, afraid that Adams would kill him."

"Somethin' stupid?" Bellows asked. "Like what?"

"Maybe he looked the other way while somebody went
into their rooms," Atwater said. "Or worse, he let them in."

"For what reason?"

Atwater shrugged.

"To rob them?" He looked at Edwards. "Did you and
Fester go into their rooms?"

"No!"

"Tell the truth," Bellows said. "You tryin' to make some extra money by robbin' their rooms?"

"I said no," Edward said. "We been followin' them all day."

Bellows looked at Atwater.

"So somebody else went through their rooms?"

"Maybe," Atwater said. "It's not important. Pull your men off them."

"Why?"

"They'll probably grab them and make them talk," he said. "I don't need Adams to know I'm having him followed and watched."

Bellows looked at Edwards.

"Do it!"

"Yeah, okay," Edwards said. "Okay if I get a drink first?"

"No," Bellows said. "You can drink after you've done what I told you."

Edwards looked like he was going to argue, but in the end he turned and left the place.

"Clint is smart," Atwater said. "He was always smart."

"I guess we better hope he's not smarter than you," Bellows said.

"He thinks I'm the same man I was in Andersonville," Atwater said. "By the time he finds out how wrong he is, it'll be too late."

# THIRTY

Clint took Molly's dress off, then removed his own clothes. They made love with both of their guns nearby.

Clint kept her on her back, determined to make her feel more than she ever had before. He knew most men were selfish lovers, so he was determined to show her that he was not like most men.

"Clint—" she started, trying to sit up.

"Shh," he said, "just lie still. I'll do all the work."

"B-But why?"

"Because I want to."

She settled onto her back.

"I never had a man say that to me before," she admitted.

"Time for a new experience, then," he said, kneading the muscles in her thighs.

"Oooh my," she said, "that feels *soooo* good."

"Turn over," he said, and she obeyed. He continued to knead her thighs from the back, then worked his hands up to her buttocks.

"Oh God," she said, "could it be that this is even better than sex?"

"I don't know," he said. "You'll have to tell me . . . later."

"Where did you learn how to do this?" she asked.

"I think the origin is China," Clint said, "but I had it done a couple of times when I was in New York."

"Oooh, it's wonderful."

He continued up to her back, rubbed her shoulders and neck, then worked his way back down again. He went all the way to her feet, rubbed them, digging his thumbs into her soles.

"Mmmmmm," Molly moaned.

Clint worked his way back up her thighs to her buttocks again, then spread her legs so he could slide his hands between her thighs. He reached beneath her, found her pussy, which was wet and already soaking the sheet. When he touched her there, she started and said, "Oh!"

"Sorry," he said, "were you asleep?"

"Oh no," she said as he slid the tip of one finger up and down her moist slit, "and I definitely am not asleep now. And you know what?"

"What?" Slowly, he slipped a finger inside her.

"As wonderful as that was, I can tell it's definitely not better than sex."

He smiled, slapped her bare ass with one hand.

When Edwards returned to Fester across the street from the hotel, Fester said, "It's about time."

"Let's go," Edwards said.

"Whataya mean?"

"We're done."

"For tonight?"

"For good, I think," Edwards said. "Bellows and Atwater think we been spotted. They don't want Adams comin' after us."

"Well, hell," Fester said, "neither do I. Let's get the hell out of here!"

# THIRTY-ONE

Because she was so wet and ready, Clint decided not to waste any more time. He got on the bed with Molly, slid his penis between her thighs. She lifted her belly off the bed to give him access and he slid right up into her. She got to her knees and moaned as he started moving in and out of her, holding her by the hips. She caught his rhythm and began to bump back into him as he came forward.

They moved slowly, almost languidly, just enjoying each other. She was so slick and hot, and he moved so easily in and out of her, that at one point he decided to try to find some more friction. He withdrew, spread her ass cheeks, and pressed the swollen head of his slickened penis to her little butt hole. If she'd resisted, he would have stopped, but she did not protest at all. He pressed forward, allowed the head of his penis to pop in, and then slowly slid the length of his penis into her.

When he started to move this time, he felt the friction he had been looking for. She groaned out loud, sought his rhythm again, found it, and started moving with him. He took her by the hips again, then slid one hand beneath her, touched her belly, then found her wet pussy again and began to stroke her as he fucked her from behind. Her breath began to come in ragged gasps, and he then felt her entire body begin to tremble beneath him. When she exploded, she bucked wildly and he tried his best to stay with her . . .

"Jesus," she said later, still lying on her stomach, "first you relax every muscle in my body, and then you do that!"

"I was just trying to give you something you'd remember," he said. He got off the bed. "I'll be right back."

"Where are you going?"

"Just across the hall."

He pulled on his pants, grabbed his gun, and went to the room across from them. In the dark he made his way to the window. He waited for his eyes to get used to the dark then looked across the street where the two men had been watching from. After a few minutes he was convinced they were no longer there.

They were either in the hotel, or they had simply left.

He hoped it was the latter.

When he returned to the room, she had rolled over onto her back. She had one leg bent, knee up, so he could see her pussy, and she was absently stroking one of her own breasts, teasing the nipple—and him.

"So?"

"They're not there."

"Where are they?"

"Either gone," he said, "or on their way up here."

She abandoned her teasing position and sat up.

"Do you think?" she asked.

"Maybe."

"Damn it."

She started to get out of bed, grabbed for her gun.

"Stay here," he said. "I'll take a look."

"But Clint—"

"Stay," he said. "No point in you getting dressed if they're gone. And if that's the case, we might be able to relax a little."

"Jesus," she said, sitting back down, "if you relaxed me any more . . ."

He slipped out of the room again and down the hall toward the stairs. He listened intently, heard nothing. He crept halfway down the stairs and saw that the lobby was empty. Still no clerk. He went back upstairs.

He slipped back into the room and said, "Unless they're hiding in one of the other rooms, they're gone."

"We have all the keys."

"That's right," Clint said. "To get into a room, they would have had to force the door."

"And we would've heard them."

He nodded.

"So they're gone?" she asked. "Why would they decide to stop watching now?"

"Maybe they're going to get some sleep and come back in the morning."

He walked to the bed and slid his gun back in its holster. He sat down on the bed. She came up behind him, crushed her breasts against his back. The nipples were pleasantly hard.

"So what do we do now?" she asked.

"Like I said," he replied, "relax for a while."

"I think," she said, dragging him down onto his back, "it's time for you to relax . . ."

# THIRTY-TWO

She slid around him so she could slip his pants off again, then straddled him and began to kiss his neck, his chest, his belly. She slithered down to pepper his groin with hot kisses. She kissed all around his penis without touching it, but it kept swelling nevertheless. When he thought he couldn't take it any more, she suddenly grasped it and began to stroke it.

With her other hand, she rubbed his thighs, reached up to rub his chest, even cupped his testicles. She pressed his hard penis to her face, rubbing it against her cheeks, moving it over her mouth, which she kept closed. She smiled, though, knowing that he was waiting for her hot mouth to take him inside.

Let him wait, she thought. Let him wonder when it would happen.

She continued to rub him with her right hand, stroke him with her left, smiling the whole time . . .

Clint reclined on his back, enjoying the feel of her hands on him, the way she rubbed his dick over her face. She slid up on him, took him between her chubby breasts, and rubbed him there. And then just what he was waiting for . . . Her hot breath on him, her lips, moist now, then her tongue, and finally the heat enveloped him, took him inside—all of him—and she began to suck . . She suckled him for a long time, enjoying how slick he felt when he was wet with her salia, then released him and scooted up on him so she could take him into her pussy, with heat even more intense than her mouth.

She caught her breath as she sank down on him, taking him in, and then began to ride him up and down. He put his hands on her hips and began to move in time with her. She leaned over to tease him with her breasts, and he licked and bit them as she dangled them in his face.

She sat up straight then, placing her hands on his chest as she continued to move on him, grinding now, seeking her release. Her eyes were closed, her head thrown back as she chased it, and then suddenly there it was, warming her, shaking her, washing over her. She opened her mouth and released a long, guttural groan . . .

To Clint it was like having molten lava rush over his crotch. She gushed, wetting him, warming him, making him sticky, exciting him more and more until finally he lifted his hips and spurted inside her, again and again, until it felt like she was milking him, until the pleasure mixed with pain, a pain he hoped would never stop . . .

She collapsed on him as he filled her with hot needles, and at one point the two of them simply twitched, no longer able to move. Breathing both hurt and felt good. Perspiration caused their skin to stick together and the room smelled of both of them.

And they fell asleep that way, with her lying on top of him, but each still aware that their guns were close by, if needed . . .

# THIRTY-THREE

They slept 'til morning, then rolled apart and groped for their clothes and guns.

"Whoa," she said when she tried to stand up.

"What?"

"My legs are weak."

He stood up.

"Mine, too. We're going to have to cut that out."

"I don't think so," she said. "It feels too good."

"Anybody could have sneaked up on us last night," he said.

"I don't think that's true either," she said. "I was very alert for trouble."

"Yeah," he said, "right."

They took turns at the pitcher and basin, but what they really needed was a bath.

"Let's have breakfast, then we'll go looking for some new clothes, and a bath," he suggested.

"Oooh, a bath together?" she said.

"No, separately, "he said, "or we'll never get out of the tub. You want to look like a prune?"

"Okay, okay," she said. "Let's go and eat."

Clint strapped on his gun belt and Molly handed him her Colt.

"Can you carry that for me?"

He tucked it into his belt. They left the room and went downstairs. There was a clerk behind the desk, but not the one they had been dealing with. This was an older man, who regarded them with a bored look as they approached.

"Rooms six and seven," Clint said. "Any telegrams for us?"

"Yes, sir," the man said. "One for six, two for seven." He handed them over.

"Thank you."

"Sir?"

"Yes?"

"Do you know what happened to our clerk?"

"No idea," Clint said. "When we came in last night, he wasn't here."

"And our keys?" the man asked. "Would you know what happened to all our keys?"

"No idea."

"Strange."

"You're not the owner, are you?" Clint asked.

"No, sir," the man said. "I'm just a clerk."

"Well, I guess you better get to finding your keys," Clint said. "Thanks for the telegrams."

"Yes, sir," the man said. "They came in this morning, sir."

Outside Molly asked, "Are we gonna read them?"

"Let's find a place for breakfast first."

"Someplace nicer than the Barbary Coast?"

Clint answered "There's a place a few blocks from here that does great steak and eggs."

"Fine," she said. "Sounds good. Lead the way."

\* \* \*

Clint tucked the three telegrams into his shirt pocket. The place was still there, and still served great steak and eggs, which they both ordered. Over coffee he handed her the telegram that was addressed to her, from Jim West. He opened his two and read what Rick Hartman and Talbot Roper had to say.

By the time they were done reading, their plates had arrived. They started eating before they discussed the contents of the telegrams.

"So?" she asked.

"I got the same from both of them," he said. "Tate's military career is stalled. He's not expected to rise any higher in rank, or position."

"That's what Jim says," she said. "But he also said he has no reason to question Tate's loyalty to the United States."

"That doesn't matter," Clint said. "Even a madman can think he's serving his country."

"You think Tate might be mad?"

"No."

"It would make sense," she said. "Didn't some men come out of Andersonville crazy?"

"Yes," he said, "some. Not Tate. Even if he's mad now, I wouldn't blame it on Andersonville. Not all these years later."

"What about Atwater? He could have come out crazy and hidden it all these years. Maybe thinking he saw Henry Wirz brought it out."

"Maybe," Clint said.

"Nothing more helpful in your telegrams?"

"No," Clint said.

She handed hers across to him.

"Jim says to telegraph a man named Frank Harper in Washington," she said. "He says he'll know more about the senator's schedule."

"Frank Harper used to be a partner of Jim's," he said. "We'll do that after we eat."

"After we have a bath and get some new clothes," she said.

"Okay," he said, tucking the telegrams away. "For now let's stop talking and start eating."

"I won't argue with that," she said.

Clint cut into his steak, scooped up some eggs, and forked the whole thing into his mouth. He was feeling stronger already.

# THIRTY-FOUR

They found a bathhouse off the Barbary Coast, just to be fairly certain their belongings—or at least, their guns and money—wouldn't be stolen while they were bathing. Clint also had a shave and a haircut before they were done.

After that they went to a store where they could both buy some new clothes. They both shopped in a similar fashion—new pants and several shirts. Molly bought a new hat. Their boots were in good shape, so neither bought any footwear. Clint bought some new socks.

They threw out their old clothes and wore some of the new duds out, carrying the rest wrapped in brown paper and tied with twine.

"Now what?" she asked.

"I think," he said, "it's probably time to change hotels. Too many people seem to know about the Bucket of Blood."

"Should we go back there?" she asked. "Your saddlebags are still there."

"With an extra gun, a book, and not much else," he said.

"What about your rifle?"

"I'll go back later," he said. "When this is all over."

"So we go to a new hotel right now?"

"Yup," he said. "Right now."

"Where?"

"I'll show you."

As they approached the Farrell House Hotel, Molly gasped. "Whooee."

"And this is off Portsmouth Square," he said. "A few blocks that way are the really big hotels and gaming houses."

"This isn't big?"

"This is considered medium," he said. "Come on, let's go inside."

As they entered the opulent lobby, she asked, "Who owns this place?"

"A good friend of mine named Duke Farrell," Clint said. He didn't bother telling her that he owned a piece of it, too.

As they approached the desk, he saw that the clerk was a stranger to him. Personnel changed constantly in the hotel business. The handsome young man watched as they walked toward him, his eyes roaming up and down Molly's body. When they stopped, she gave him a hard stare.

"Can I help you, sir?" he asked. "Ma'am?"

"Yes," Clint said, "is Duke around?"

"Mr. Farrell is in his office," the young man said. "Can I say—"

"I know the way," Clint said. "Thanks."

"Sir, you can't—"

"Don't worry, son," Clint said. "It's okay. We're old friends."

He led Molly down a hallway with the young clerk still stammering behind them. When he reached the office door, he knocked and then opened it. Duke Farrell looked up from his desk.

"So, you finally gave up on your Barbary Coast palace?" he asked.

"Yep," Clint said. "We need a room, Duke. Got anything available?"

Farrell smiled and said, "Best room in the house, for you."

He came around the desk and the two men embraced warmly. Farrell was barely five-foot-five, but he was a big man in Clint's eyes. As always, he was wearing a very expensive suit, and his haircut was recent and impeccable.

"Duke, this is Molly."

"Hello, Molly. You smell mighty good."

"Just had a bath," she said. "It's nice to meet you, Mr. Farrell."

"Duke," Farrell said, "just call me Duke."

"Okay, Duke."

Farrell looked at Clint. The smaller man could have been forty or fifty, Clint had never known his true age. He had spent many years as a con man before becoming a hotel owner.

"I got your message," Farrell said. "Did I help?"

"You helped a lot, but now I need a room here."

"You've always got a room here, Clint," Farrell said. "You know that."

"Thanks, Duke."

"Want to tell me what it's about?" Farrell asked.

"Not yet."

"Am I gonna get shot at? Or arrested?"

"Shot at, maybe," Clint said, "but not arrested."

"Well, that's somethin'," Farrell said. "Come on, let's get you that room."

Out in the lobby Farrell introduced Clint and Molly to the desk clerk, whose name was Cal.

"Mr. Adams has a regular room in the hotel, Cal," Farrell said. "The key's always in the upper-left-hand slot."

"That's the one you tell me never to rent out," Cal said.

"That's right."

"So this is . . ." Cal said, indicating Clint.

"Yes," Molly said, "he's the Gunsmith."

Cal, about Molly's age, looked at her and asked, "And who are you?"

"For now," she said, "I'm with him."

"So," Cal asked, "one room, then?"

"That's right," Molly said brazenly, "one room."

Cal looked at Clint.

"Any luggage?"

"Sure." Clint picked up the two brown paper bundles they'd put down when they first came in and handed them to the clerk. "There you go. Take them upstairs like a good lad."

"I'm a desk clerk," Cal said, "not a bell man."

"Take them upstairs, Cal," Farrell said. "We'll talk later."

"Sure, boss."

Cal came around the desk and took the bundles up the stairs with him.

"Dining room's open," Farrell said. "Want to get a bite to eat?"

"Coffee'd be good," Clint said.

"I think I'll go up to the room," Molly said. "See you there later."

"Sure," Clint said.

As she went up the stairs, Farrell noticed the Colt Paterson in her belt.

"Will she shoot Cal?" he asked.

"Only if he gets fresh," Clint said.

Farrell smiled and said, "I guess he's as good as dead, then. Come on, let's get that coffee. I think I should hear more about what might get me shot at."

"But not arrested," Clint reminded him.

# THIRTY-FIVE

"She's a what?" Farrell asked.

"A Secret Service agent."

Farrell sat back in his chair.

"You're kiddin'."

"I'm not."

"How old is she?"

"I never asked."

"Are you workin' for the Secret Service now?" Farrell asked.

"Not in any official capacity," Clint said. "I just happened to end up with her."

"So who are you workin' for?"

"I'm doin' a favor for somebody."

"Don't tell me, let me guess," Farrell said. "West?"

Clint nodded.

"That jasper is always gettin' you in trouble."

"We've gotten each other into a lot of trouble over the years."

"You and me?"

"Me and him," Clint said, "but yeah, you and me, too."

"What's goin' on, Clint?"

Clint had never told Farrell about Andersonville, and he wasn't going to start now. At the moment Molly was the only person he'd ever told, and he wanted to keep it that way. He'd never mentioned it to Bat Masterson, Wyatt Earp, Rick Hartman, Talbot Roper—none of them. Jim West knew, but that was different.

"What do you know about a U.S. senator named Harlan Winston?"

"Shitkicker politician from the South," Farrell said. "Got elected on the basis of his accent, I think."

Clint sat back. It sounded like Farrell knew more than anyone else he'd inquired with.

"Go on."

"I don't know much more," Farrell said. "I just never knew how he got elected. One minute he was nobody—no, 'unknown' would be a better word—and the next thing you know, he's in the Senate."

"Just like that?"

"Just like that," Farrell said. "If I didn't know any better, I'd say the fix was in."

"Why wouldn't you say the fix is in?" Clint asked.

"Because we all know elections aren't fixed, right?" Farrell asked.

Clint didn't respond. What if the fix had been in? But who fixed it? And why? And if there was a fix, that didn't mean that Winston was Henry Wirz.

"You want to tell me what this is all really about?" Farrell asked.

"Nope," Clint said. "Better for you not to know."

"So from this point on, I should just mind my own business?"

"That would be best, Duke."

Farrell sat back.

"I'm gonna have some pie."

"Peach?" Clint asked.

"Apple," Farrell said, "but I can get you peach if you want."

"Okay," Clint said. "I'll have a piece of pie with you."

Farrell waved the waiter over.

In the hallway upstairs Molly had been heading for the room when the door opened and Cal stepped out.

"Where's your Gunsmith?" he asked.

"Downstairs with your boss," she said.

He blocked her path.

"So I guess that leaves you and me."

She laughed. He crowded her against the wall.

"I don't think that's very likely," she said.

"Why not?"

"Because you said it yourself," she answered. "You're a desk clerk."

"And he's a cheap gunman."

"There's nothing cheap about Clint Adams."

She tried to spin away from him, but he put his hand on her arm.

"If you don't move that hand, you'll lose it."

"I'm not used to having girls tell me to take my hands off them," he said.

Her hand came around from behind her back and she shoved the barrel of the Colt Paterson underneath his chin.

"This *woman* is telling you to move your hand."

He removed it.

"Now you better go back to work while you still can."

She could see that he wanted to say something, but in the end he just turned and stormed away.

When Clint came up to the room, Molly had made herself comfortable. She was sitting in an overstuffed armchair, drinking brandy from a snifter.

"This is better than any room I ever saw in a Washington hotel," she said.

"Glad you like it."

He sat in the other chair.

"Did you get anything from your friend?"

"Not much."

"So what's our next step?"

"I'm stuck."

"What?"

"I don't know what to do next."

"So we just wait for the senator to arrive next Tuesday?"

"I suppose."

"That'll be your first look at him, right?"

"Yes."

"And you'll be able to tell whether or not he's Wirz?" she asked.

"Hopefully."

"And if he is, you've got a whole new problem."

"Let's just cross that bridge when we come to it," he said.

"Too bad you can't get a look at him before that," she said.

Clint sat up in his chair.

"What is it?"

"Photographs."

"What about them?"

"He's a U.S. senator," he said. "There must be photographs of him somewhere."

"Like a newspaper?" she asked.

"Exactly."

"So we go back and see Atwater?" she asked.

"No," he said, "we go and see Gates."

# THIRTY-SIX

Atwater looked up and saw Bellows standing in front of his desk.

"What are you doing here?"

Bellows sat down.

"Adams and the girl have left the Bucket of Blood," Bellows said.

"So?"

"Do you know where they are?"

"Why would I know?"

"We have to find out," Bellows said. "We can't have them running around loose."

"Why not? What can they do? They don't know anything," Atwater pointed out.

"They know that Winston is Wirz," Bellows said.

"No, they know that I think Winston is Wirz," Atwater said. "And I'm just a drunken newspaperman, remember?"

"We should get rid of him."

"Kill the Gunsmith?" Atwater said, laughing. "Which of you is man enough to try that?"

Bellows didn't answer.

"Look," Atwater said, "keep an eye on me and you'll find them again."

"Hey, that's a good idea," Bellows said. "They'll have to come back and talk to you."

"If only to get me to admit I'm wrong."

"I'll have Fester or Edwards watch you."

"Those two idiots," Atwater said. "Whichever one it is, make sure you tell them to stay away from me. I don't want to be seen with them."

"Right."

"Or with you," the newspaperman said, "so get out of here."

"You're a big talker, Atwater," Bellows said, "knowing that you ain't the one who's gonna pull the trigger on Winston."

"Who knows?" Atwater said. "Maybe I am."

Bellows didn't know what to say to that, so he got up and left.

Once Bellows was gone, Atwater sat back in his chair. Something had been bothering him. Questions.

If the government had sent Clint Adams to stop him, why hadn't they just arrested him for threatening the senator?

Or why not just warn the senator himself? Or bring a battalion of soldiers to San Francisco?

He could only think of one answer.

Adams hadn't been sent by the government. He'd been sent by one man.

But who?

One man who worked for the senator? No, if Adams had seen Senator Winston, he'd know the same thing Atwater knew, that it was Wirz.

No, Clint Adams had never seen the senator. He'd only seen the man who sent him here.

Who was it?

In the end, it didn't actually matter who it was. Because it was going to take more than one man to stop Dorence Atwater.

# THIRTY-SEVEN

"Back again?" Gates asked as Clint and Molly entered his office. "What can I do for you this time? I was just about to head home."

"I need a favor, Larry."

"What kind of favor?"

"Photographs."

"Wonderful invention," Gates said. "What about them?"

"I need to see some photographs of Senator Winston," Clint said. "This is a newspaper. You must have some on hand."

Gates sat back in his chair.

"Maybe I do," he said, "but what do I get for showing them to you?"

"I told you," Clint said. "If there's a story, it's yours."

"That's not good enough."

"What do you want, Larry?" Molly asked.

He looked at her.

"An interview," he said, then looked at Clint. "With you."

"I told you—"

"You don't do interviews," Gates said. "I know. I remember. But you do want to see photographs of the senator, right?"

"Yes."

"Why?"

Clint shrugged.

"I've never seen the man before."

"There's got to be a better reason than that," Gates said. "Shall I guess?"

"What would be your guess?" Molly asked.

Gates pressed his fingertips together and regarded Clint for a moment.

"How about this?" he said. "When you see a photograph of the senator, you expect to recognize him."

Molly looked startled, then looked over at Clint.

"How am I doing?" Gates asked.

"Okay," Clint said.

"Okay . . . what?"

"You've got your interview."

Gates started to get up, then sat back down.

"What's wrong?" Clint asked.

"I just thought of something."

"What?"

"What happens if you end up dead?"

"Then we both lose," Clint said, "and you don't get your interview."

Gates told Clint it would take some time to find the photographs, but Clint said they'd wait. While they waited, everyone else left for the day, until it was only Clint and Molly in the office.

"He must be having trouble finding them," she said.

"Or there are so many of them," Clint said.

They waited awhile longer.

"Okay," she said, "now it's too long."

"Let's go."

They left Gates's office and started walking around the building, trying to find him. They opened and closed doors on other offices.

"A different floor?" she asked.

"I don't like this," he said, putting his hand on his gun.

Molly knew she couldn't snake her gun from her belt as fast as Clint could from his holster, so she palmed it right away.

"End of the hall," he said.

There was a door marked MORGUE.

"Dead people?" she asked.

"No," he said, "dead newspapers."

They crept down the hall until they reached the door. Clint put his hand on the doorknob and turned it. When he opened it, he sniffed the air and cursed.

"What"

"That smell?"

She sniffed.

"I don't—"

"It's blood," he said.

They stepped into the room. There was a light burning, though not very bright. From the glow, though, they could see Larry Gates lying on the floor, with his throat cut.

"Damn it!" Clint said.

"Who—" Molly started.

"Forget it," Clint said. "Whoever killed him is long gone."

"But why?"

"The photographs," Clint said. "I'll bet they're all gone, too."

"But who knew—"

Clint noticed that Gates's right hand was closed into a fist. He leaned over him, avoiding the blood on the floor as best he could, and forced the hand open. In it he found a crumpled photograph.

"Is that—" Molly asked.

"Yes," Clint said. "One photograph the killer missed."

"Who is it?"

Clint uncrumpled it. It was not a good photograph, and the light was too dim.

"We'll look at it later," he said, putting it in his pocket. "For now let's get out of here."

"What about the police?"

"We'll send word to them," he said, "but I don't want to get tangled up with them. Come on, Molly. We have to go."

"Funny," she said as they hurried back up the hall.

"What is?"

"You didn't end up dead," she said, "he did."

"But we both still lost."

# THIRTY-EIGHT

Molly wasn't comfortable with leaving the body behind and not waiting for the police.

"Look, we had nothing to do with his murder, but the police might not see it that way," Clint said. "And you might have to call your bosses in to get us out. And knowing your bosses—or at least some of the past bosses of the Secret Service—I know they don't want to have to do that."

"You're probably right," she said grudgingly.

"When we get back to the hotel, we'll send word to the police so they can discover Gates's body and start working on who killed him."

"Should we get a cab?" she asked.

"No," he said, "the police will be checking with every cab to see if they picked anyone up in this area. Let's walk as far as we can."

"What about that photograph?" she asked. "Let's get a look at it."

"Let's walk further, then we'll find a saloon or something to duck into, and we'll take a look."

She had to walk very quickly to keep up with his long strides.

When Clint felt they were far enough away from the offices of the *Examiner*, they did, indeed, duck into a small café. It was apparently filled with regulars, who all turned and looked at them when they entered.

"Great," Clint said.

"Maybe they're just looking at me?" she suggested.

"That would be good. There's a table over there," he said, jerking his chin.

It was not in the back of the room, but it was against one wall.

A comely waitress with lots of blond ringlets and a low-cut peasant blouse came over, gave Clint a look up and down, and then asked, "What can I get you?"

"Coffee for me," Clint said.

"And me."

"Comin' up."

As she walked away, Molly said to Clint, "Let's see it."

Clint took it out of his pocket and smoothed it out. It was not a photograph, but a clip that had been torn from a newspaper.

"Can you make it out?"

It was a head and shoulders shot, and beneath it were the words "Senator Harlan Winston." It measured only about three inches by three inches and was creased in many places.

"He had it clutched in his hand," Clint said, "so he was definitely hiding it."

"But it's all creased."

Clint placed it on the table and tried to smooth it out.

"Can you recognize him?" Molly asked. "Is it Henry Wirz?"

Clint stared at it intently. The man in the photograph was

in his sixties, and even though it was a black-and-white photograph, he could see the man had white hair beneath a hat. There was also a white mustache.

"Wirz was clean shaven," Clint said. "This man is so much older." He sat back, frustrated. "Damn it, Gates died for nothing. I can't tell from this picture."

The waitress came with their coffee, thought about flirting with Clint, but decided against it when she saw the expression on his face.

"Bad news, honey?" she asked Molly.

"The worst."

"Want somethin' stronger than coffee?"

"No," Molly said, "this'll do for now. Thanks."

Clint picked up the coffee cup and absently sipped from it.

"Goddamnit, I thought this was going to solve some of our problems," he said.

Molly turned the photograph around so she could look at it, but she didn't know what she was looking at, having never seen Henry Wirz before.

"So we're back where we started," she said. "We have to wait for the senator to get here."

"Looks like it."

"And what do we do until then?"

"I'll tell you what I'd like to do," Clint said. "Find the sonofabitch who cut Larry Gates's throat."

"That would mean going to the police and trying to help them. And we don't want to do that," she reminded him.

"I know."

"So we're stuck."

"Looks like it."

"Maybe," she said, waving to the waitress, "we *should* have something stronger."

# THIRTY-NINE

When they got back to the hotel, Clint had to tell Duke Farrell that Gates was dead.

"Okay," Farrell said, sitting behind his desk, "now you owe me an explanation."

Clint hesitated. How much did he want to tell his friend?

"I'm here to make sure nobody kills Senator Winston when he comes to town next week," Clint said.

"What did Gates have to do with that?"

"I needed some information on a local, another newspaperman."

"Who?"

"His name's Dorence Atwater, works for a newspaper called *The Reporter*."

"That's a rag. Did you know Gates worked with Mark Twain?"

"So he told me," Clint said. "Look, we need to get word to the police, but I need to stay out of it."

"I'll pass the word," Farrell said.

Farrell turned to Molly. "What about the Secret Service? Can they do something?"

"The Secret Service does not want to get involved with the local police," Molly said.

"And who can blame them," Farrell said. "Our police are not as corrupt as they used to be, but everything is relative. How about a drink? You both look like you could use one. I have cognac and whiskey here, or we could get beer from the bar."

Farrell stood up and moved to a sideboard with bottles on it.

"Cognac for me," Clint said.

"Whiskey," Molly said. She seemed more upset about finding Gates's body than Clint was.

Farrell poured two glasses and handed them to his guests, then poured a cognac for himself and sat back down behind his desk.

"So we're tryin' to avert an assassination?"

That sounded as good a way as any to explain everything to Farrell, so Clint said, "Yes, we are."

"Any idea who the potential assassin is?"

"No," Molly said, "we only got word that somebody was planning to try when the senator got here."

"So don't let the senator come here," he suggested. "Oh, wait, I'll bet you've already proposed that and been turned down."

"Oh, yes."

"That figures. That would be much too easy an answer, wouldn't it?"

"For the government?" Clint asked. "Yes."

"So what's your next step?" Farrell asked. "Whatever you were getting from Larry, can you get it from someone else?"

"I don't want to risk anyone else's life," Clint said. "That includes you, Duke."

"So you still want me to butt out?"

"Definitely."

"Then what are you going to do?"

"We were being followed for a while," Clint said, looking at Molly. "Maybe it's time to find out who that was."

"Why didn't you find out before, when you realized you were being followed?" Farrell asked.

"That's a good question," Clint said. "I think I waited too long, and suddenly they were gone."

"How do you intend to find them again?"

"I'm hoping," Clint said, "they'll find us again."

Clint and Molly left Farrell's office, and instead of going back to their room, they went to the dining room. For some reason they were both famished just shortly after finding a dead body.

"This makes me feel like a ghoul," Molly said, cutting into a steak.

"People react differently to finding bodies," he said. "Don't feel bad. Just feed the feeling."

They ate in silence for a while, alone with their thoughts, before Molly asked, "How do we make them find us again, Clint?"

"I'm not sure," he said, "but we noticed them after we talked with Atwater."

"So we go back to him?"

"What else do we have?" he asked. "We know it's Dorence who's planning to kill the senator. We need to find out who he has helping him, and whether or not they killed Gates."

"Maybe hearing that Gates—another newspaperman— was killed will shake him up," she suggested.

"Let's find out tomorrow," he said.

"So what do we do tonight?"

"I think tonight," he said after a moment, "I'll take you gambling."

# FORTY

In order to go to some of the gambling halls in Portsmouth Square, they had to buy something else for Molly to wear. There was a dress shop down the street they managed to get to before it closed. There was no time for the seamstress to make something for her, but they managed to find something hanging on a rack that would fit her.

They took the gown back to the room. Farrell was able to supply Clint with a suit to wear. After he'd donned it, he went down to the lobby to wait for Molly. Farrell waited with him.

"Do you think a night on the town is in order?" he asked.

"I think she might need it," Clint said. "I don't think she's found many bodies."

"But she's Secret Service."

"I'm not sure how long she's been in the service," Clint said.

"Wow!"

They turned. It was Cal who had spoken. They followed his gaze and saw Molly coming down the stairs in the gown.

It didn't fit perfectly—it was a bit too small—but it certainly showed off her attributes. Her shoulders were bare, breasts pushed together and up, which seemed to embarrass her. The color of the gown—jade green—seemed to show off her skin and her red hair well.

"I—I can't go out like this," she said. "I feel . . . naked."

"Wait," Farrell said. "Cal—"

"I got you, boss."

Cal reached beneath the desk and came out with a green shawl.

"A lady left this here last week. We've been waiting for her to come back for it," Farrell said. "I don't think she'd mind if you used it."

Cal handed it to Molly, who draped it over her shoulders. It effectively covered her shoulders and cleavage.

"Is that better?" Clint asked.

"How does it look?" she asked.

"It's not an exact match of the green, but it will do," Clint said. "You look lovely."

"Yes, indeed," Farrell said.

Cal had gone back behind the desk, but was staring at Molly, so he seemed to agree.

"Shall we go?" Clint asked.

"Where exactly?" she asked.

"Portsmouth Square," he said. "The Alhambra, Parker House, the Bella Union, the Empire, the Arcade, as many of the others as we can get to in one night."

"One night," Molly said.

"And then it's back to work," Clint said. "Agreed?"

She smiled at him and said, "Agreed."

He put his arm out and she took it.

"I have a hansom cab waiting for you out front," Farrell said.

"But . . . I thought it was only blocks away," she said.

"It is," Farrell said, "but a woman who looks the way

you do should arrive in Portsmouth Square in style, don't you think?"

"I think so, too," Clint said.

They walked out the door arm in arm.

# FORTY-ONE

Clint took Molly to several of the gambling palaces and they ended up at the Alhambra. She had never gambled before so he showed her how to play blackjack and faro and roulette.

She decided she liked roulette so Clint gave her some money to play with. She clapped happily when she played a number and it came up. She then kept playing the number over and over and eventually lost all the money she had won when the number hit.

"Do you want to play some more?" he asked.

"I don't think so."

He took her to a table and they ordered drinks from a beautiful saloon girl.

"So that's gambling?" she asked.

"That's gambling," he said, nodding, "but that's bad gambling."

"Bad?"

"You could have walked away from the table ahead, but you decided to keep playing until you had lost all the money back."

"And I shouldn't have done that."

"You definitely shouldn't have done that," he said.

"What should I have done?"

"You should have kept winning."

She frowned at him.

"What am I supposed to feel, now that I've gambled?" she asked.

"Well," he said, "if you enjoyed it, you should feel . . . elated."

"And if I didn't enjoy it?"

"Then you'd feel . . . empty."

She paused for a moment, then said, "Well, when my number came up on the wheel, I felt elated, but when I lost back all the money I had won, I felt . . . empty."

"And what do you feel now?"

She pulled her shawl closer and said, "Cold."

"Maybe we should call it a night."

She looked around at the other women in the room, most of whom were wearing gowns similar to hers, some more expensive, some even more revealing.

"They don't seem to mind walking around . . . un-covered."

When she looked at him, he was staring at her.

"All right," she said, "so I'm a little less . . . experienced than I claim to be."

"How long have you been with the Secret Service?" he asked.

"Eight months."

"And in that time you've worked with Jim?"

"Several times."

"Then you've learned a lot."

"I haven't learned to . . . dress right, or act right in certain situations."

"You will."

"But there are certain situations I do know how to act right in," she said, staring at him suggestively.

"Yes," he said, "I've noticed."

"Why don't we go back to the room?" she suggested.

"Sure," Clint said, "why don't we?"

He paid for the drinks and they got up and headed for the door. On the way Clint thought he saw a man he knew going out the door ahead of them.

"Come on," he said, "hurry."

"Clint—" she said, but he pulled her along.

They hurried out the front door, where he saw the man get into a cab. He grabbed the doorman and asked him to get them a cab, fast.

"What's going on?" she asked.

"The man who got into that cab," he said, pointing. "I know him."

"From where?"

The doorman came back and said he had a cab for them.

"Come on!"

He pulled Molly to the cab, where they got in and he told the driver to go.

"Where?" the man asked.

"Follow that cab."

"Which one?"

"The one that just left."

The driver flicked the reins at his horse and it went off at a trot.

"Which way did he go?" the driver asked.

"I don't know," Clint said. "He went straight, I guess."

"I see a cab ahead," the driver said, "but I don't know if it's the one you want."

"Well, just keep going and let's find out," Clint said.

"It's dark," the driver said, "but I'll try to stay with him."

"I'll pay you well if you do."

That made the man flick his reins with that much more sharpness.

Molly, sitting across from him, sat forward and slapped him on the leg.

"Will you tell me who we're chasing?"

"That soldier," Clint said, snapping his fingers.

"Which soldier?"

"Uh . . . Private Collins," Clint said, "the soldier who was with Tate when we saw him on the train."

"That man is Collins?" she said. "Then that means Colonel Tate is in town?"

"I don't know what it means," Clint said, "but I intend to find out."

# FORTY-TWO

They followed the cab ahead of them for street after street until Clint finally decided they should just stop him.

"How do I do that?" the driver asked.

"Get ahead of him," Clint said. "Tell him to pull over. Don't you know who he is? He's another driver, isn't he?"

"Yes, he is," the driver called over his shoulder. "But that doesn't mean I know him."

"Don't you both pick up fares in front of the hotels?" Clint asked.

"Yes, we do, but that's not one of the cabs from the Square."

"What?"

"I know the names of the other drivers."

"That's not the cab that was just ahead of you in front of the Alhambra?"

"No, sir, it ain't. I'd recognize it if it was."

"Then where's that one?"

"I don't know."

"But you know who drives it?"

"Sure," the man said, "that's Andy's cab."

"And that's not Andy's cab," Clint said, pointing.

"No, it ain't," the man said. "That's what I'm telling' you!"

"Can you pass him?"

"Can I?" the guy said. "I got the best horse in San Francisco."

"Well, pull him over anyway," Clint said. "We might as well have a look."

"It's gonna cost you extra."

"No problem."

The driver nodded and snapped his reins so that his horse accelerated. They eventually passed the other cab, then pulled in front of it, forcing the driver to rein in his horse.

"What the hell is wrong with you?" the man shouted. "You Portsmouth Square cabs think you own the streets!"

"Relax," the driver said. "My fare just wants to take a look at yours."

Clint got out of the cab, followed by Molly, moving as quickly as she could in her gown. They ran to the other cab and looked in.

"What's going on?" the fare asked. He was a small man of about sixty. "I didn't do anything."

"It's not him," Clint said when Molly had caught up.

They turned and walked back to their cab.

"Is that it?" the other driver asked. "Can I go now?"

"Sure," Clint said, "go."

As the other cab pulled away, Clint's driver, a young man in his late twenties, said, "Where to now, boss?"

"Take us to the Farrell House Hotel. You know where that is?"

"Sure," the man said, "that's Duke's place. Hop in."

The cab dropped them in front of the Farrell House. Clint paid the cab driver, and gave him extra for his trouble.

"Thanks, mister."

"Hold on a second," Clint said as the man started to drive away. Molly waited in the doorway.

"Yeah?"

"Your buddy Andy?"

"What about him?"

"I'd like to find out where he took his fare tonight."

"Which fare?"

"The one he just took," Clint said. "Can you get him to come and see me tomorrow?"

"Are you the police?" the man asked.

"No, I'm not," Clint said. "What's your name?"

"Paul."

"Paul, I'll pay Andy to come see me, and I'll pay you to get him to come and see me."

Clint took a few dollars out and handed them to Paul.

"When?"

"Tomorrow, in the morning. You guys can both eat breakfast here, on me."

"Are you friends with Duke?"

"Yes," Clint said, "he'll vouch for me. My name's Clint Adams."

The name hit home. He could see it in Paul's face, although the younger man tried not to let it show.

"Okay, Mr. Adams," Paul said. "Tomorrow morning."

"Nine, okay?"

"Nine," Paul said, "sharp."

# FORTY-THREE

In their room the mood was pensive.

"This is why I hate getting involved with the Secret Service, or the government, or politics," Clint said.

"Why?" Molly queried.

"Because somebody's always doing something underhanded, or just flat-out lying."

"Collins?"

"Tate," Clint said. "If Collins is here, Tate knows about it. And Tate himself might be here as well."

"But why? Why would he come if he asked you to come?" Molly asked.

"That's what I want to know," he said. "And if I find out he is here, I'm out."

"What?"

"Gone," Clint said. "I'll leave town immediately."

"You don't care about the senator, or whether or not he's Wirz?"

"He's not Wirz, all right?" Clint said. "Henry Wirz is dead. He was hanged. Executed. Period. Tate used that bull about him still being alive just to get me here, and I don't like it."

"What about Jim West?" Molly asked. "Is he lying? Or doing something underhanded?"

"No," Clint said. "He simply sent me a telegram on behalf of Colonel Tate. Tate's the one playing games."

"What if you do leave San Francisco, and Atwater kills Senator Winston—whether he turns out to be Wirz or not? How would you feel then?"

"I'll feel bad," Clint said, "but it won't be my fault. I'll live with it."

She had hung her gown up and was lying in bed with the sheet pulled up to her neck. The way the sheet lay on her body made it plain she was naked.

Clint turned to look at her, wearing only his underwear.

"If you leave, you know I'll have to stay," she said. "I'll have to try and stop Atwater—and whoever's helping him—by myself."

"If Tate's here, all you have to do is make him bring some more men in," Clint said.

"If he was going to bring in more men, he would have by now."

"And how do we know he hasn't?" Clint demanded. "Collins is here. Probably Tate. And who else?"

"So then why did he want you here?"

"I'll tell you why," Clint said, sitting on the bed. "He needs a scapegoat."

"For what?"

"I don't know," Clint said, "but I've got that scapegoat feeling."

"But . . . he's your friend."

"I told you before, I knew the young Lieutenant Tate," Clint said. "We weren't friends, but I knew him. This Colonel Tate, him I don't know, and don't trust."

"Yes," she said, "you told me before you don't trust him."

"Even less now."

"What about me?" she asked. "Do you trust me yet?"

He put his hand on her leg and said, "Yes, I trust you."

That delighted her. She tossed off the sheet and threw her arms around him from behind, crushing her breasts into his back. She kissed his neck.

"Thank you," she said.

"And I won't leave you alone here," he said. "I'm just talking because I'm mad. There's no way I'd leave you to handle this alone."

She kissed his neck and said, "I know."

They got beneath the sheet, rubbed up close together, and let nature take its course.

When Molly was asleep, Clint got out of bed and went into the other room. He poured himself a brandy from the decanter and sat in one of the armchairs. He was still angry at Tate, but what if Collins was in San Francisco on his own? What if Collins was the wild card in this deck? What if he was the one who killed Gates?

But why?

It didn't make sense, unless Collins wasn't a soldier. And if he wasn't a soldier, that meant Tate wasn't one either.

The news he'd gotten about Tate was that the man had finished his assent through the ranks. Maybe Tate wasn't happy about that.

# FORTY-FOUR

Clint and Molly were downstairs in the dining room when Paul the driver came in with his friend Andy in tow. Andy was even younger than Paul, probably mid-twenties.

"Clint Adams," Paul said. "This is Andy. He picked up that fella you were talkin' about last night, outside the Alhambra."

"Skinny little fella in a suit that was too big for him?" Andy asked.

"That's him," Clint said. "Sit down, boys. Have some breakfast."

They ordered steak and eggs all around. Molly poured coffee for the two boys.

"This is Miss O'Henry," Clint said.

"Ma'am," Andy said. Paul also nodded.

"Had you seen that man before last night?" Clint asked Andy.

"No, sir."

"And did you see him arrive at the Alhambra?"

"No, sir."

Clint looked at Paul.

"I didn't drive him there, and I never seen him—still ain't. You described him to me."

"Okay," Clint said. "Where did you take him, Andy?"

"To a street corner."

"Just a corner? No building? Hotel, or anything?" Clint asked.

"No, sir," Andy said. "He told me to take him to the corner of Market and Drumm Streets."

"Where is that?"

"Down near Pier One," Paul said.

"What else is there?"

Andy shrugged. "Just buildings."

"Did you see anyone else when you dropped him off?" Clint asked.

"No, sir."

"Did he say anything else to you?"

"No, sir," Andy said, "just tol' me where to take him."

"Okay," Clint said. "Let's have our breakfast and then you can drive me down there, too."

"Sure thing," Andy said. His eyes widened—as did Paul's—when the waiter brought huge plates of steak and eggs.

Andy drove Clint and Molly to Market and Drumm Streets, where he said he'd dropped off the man Clint believed to be Collins.

Clint paid Andy and said, "Thanks, kid."

"Do you want me to stay and wait for you?" Andy asked. "It ain't no problem."

"That's okay, Andy," Clint said. "We'll be fine. Thanks."

"Sure thing," Andy said. "Ma'am."

Molly gave him a smile.

They watched as Andy drove away and then Molly turned to Clint and said, "Where to?"

Clint pointed and said, "The water."

* * *

They walked down to the end of Pier 1 without seeing anything interesting. Men were loading and unloading freight from ships, paused to give Molly and Clint a long look—probably just Molly, who was wearing trousers so she could keep her Colt tucked into her belt.

"Where could he have gone?" Molly asked.

"Anywhere," Clint said. "He might even have simply caught a second cab and had it take him to a hotel."

"To avoid being followed?"

Clint nodded.

"And it's possible it wasn't him, right?"

"Possible," Clint said, "but I'm pretty sure it was."

"What if it is him, but Colonel Tate doesn't know he's here?"

"I thought about that," Clint said. "Collins could be acting on his own."

"To do what?"

"I don't know," Clint said. "Come on, we'll walk around a bit, and then I'm going to send a telegram."

"To who?"

"The colonel," Clint said. "On the off chance he doesn't know his private is in San Francisco, I'm going to tell him."

# FORTY-FIVE

The area was mostly warehouses, and Clint knew that Private Collins could be in any one of them, or not. They could walk around and ask if anyone had seen the man, but Collins was ordinary-looking, and most of the men they saw in the area were working.

However, there was one place they might ask some questions.

"Let's try that saloon over there before we leave the area," Clint said. "Are you up for it?"

"Why wouldn't I be?" she asked.

"This is going to be a real working man's saloon, Molly," Clint said. "Dockworkers aren't used to seeing women in their bars."

"I've got my gun," she said, "and I've got you. I'm ready."

"Okay," Clint said. "Let's go."

They went over to the saloon and walked right in like they belonged there. Clint ignored the looks of the men and led Molly directly to the bar.

"Mister," the bartender—a big, burly-looking man with

a lazy eye—asked, "are you lookin' for trouble bringin' her in here?"

"No, but I am lookin' for somebody," Clint said. "In fact, two somebodies." He described to the bartender both the colonel and Private Collins, but he didn't describe either one in uniform.

"Have you seen anybody like that?"

"I see lots of men in here," the barman said. "I don't pay attention to them, only to what they drink. Now get your girlfriend out of here before one of these guys take a likin' to her and you lose her."

"Maybe," Clint said to the bartender, "I'll ask the rest of these gents if they've seen my friends."

"Look," the bartender said, "I have enough fights in here on good days. I ain't seen your friends, and neither has anybody else."

Molly was looking around the room while Clint concentrated on the bartender. She made the mistake of locking eyes with a man who was sitting in a corner with two friends. Obviously a dockworker with a cloth cap and an earring in his ear, he winked at her and grinned, showing yellow teeth where there weren't gaps.

She looked away, but it was too late. The man said something to his two friends, and the three of them got up. Clint heard the scraping of their chairs on the floor. He turned just as they reached him. The bartender reached beneath the bar, but Clint pointed at him and said, "Don't."

The bartender froze.

"What do you three want?" Clint asked.

"It ain't what we want, friend," the man with the earring said. "It's what your lady wants."

"The lady wants nothing to do with you," Clint said.

"That ain't what her eyes was sayin' a minute ago," the man said. "She was lookin' me up and down."

"I was wondering how a man so dirty could have two

friends sitting with him," she said, sniffing the air. "Now I know. You're all filthy."

"What the hell—" one of the other men said. "The bitch has a mouth on her."

"Let's teach her—" the third man said, reaching for her.

All three men moved toward Molly so Clint had no choice. He threw a punch that landed on the jaw of the man with the earring, driving him back and into an empty table, upsetting it.

The second man he kicked in the shin, and when the man howled and bent over to grab it, Clint hit him in the jaw as well. The blow knocked him to the floor, where he saw him holding his leg.

The third man froze when Molly put the barrel of her Colt Paterson underneath his chin.

"The bitch has a mouth, and a gun," she said to him, "and you're only going to get to experience the gun."

She cocked the hammer back.

"Molly!" Clint snapped. "Put it away."

The bartender started to reach under the bar again.

"I said don't!" Clint snapped, pointing his finger again. "I'm not as free with my gun as she is, but when I draw, somebody usually dies."

The bartender froze. The other men in the place froze as well, except for one, who said, "Kill him, girlie. I owe him money."

"I'm really tempted."

"We just came in here looking for information on two men," Clint said. He described both of them again in detail. "Have any of you seen one or both of them?"

There was no answer.

"I'll take that as a no," Clint said. "Molly, we're leaving. Uh, try not to kill that man unless he forces you to."

The other two men were on the floor, and were staying down, just in case she decided to kill them.

They worked their way to the door, Molly covering the room with her Colt.

Outside, Clint said, "Okay, put it away."

Molly took a deep breath and let it out.

"I wanted to kill that man."

"I could tell."

She put the gun back in her belt.

"Well, that wasn't very helpful," she said. "We didn't find out anything in there."

"Not yet."

"What do you mean?"

"I mean one of those men must know something," Clint said. "He just has to get away from the others so he can tell us."

"And how's he supposed to find us to tell us?" she asked.

"That's easy," he said. "We're going to wait for him at the end of the block."

He started walking away and she followed him, shaking her head.

# FORTY-SIX

They waited at the end of the street for ten minutes then a man came out the front door of the saloon. He looked both ways, spotted them, and came walking toward them. He didn't stop, though.

"Around the corner," he said to them as he passed.

They walked around the corner and found him waiting in the doorway of a building.

"Those two men yer lookin' for," the man said. He was obviously a dockworker, short but burly, with short black hair shot with gray.

"What about them?" Clint asked.

"You willin' ta pay?"

"Pay for what?"

"To find them!" the man said. "Whataya playin' games or somethin'?"

"We're not playing any games, mister," Clint said. "If you want to get paid, I want to know what it is I'm paying for."

"I can tell ya where ta find those two men yer lookin' fer," he said.

"And you want to tell me now and have me pay you, right?"

"Well, yeah."

"And how do I know when I get there, they'll actually be there?"

"Hey," the man said, "I'm gonna tell you where I saw them. If they ain't there when you get there, that ain't my fault."

Clint looked at Molly.

"He's got a point."

"Wait," the man said, "you want proof I saw them, right?"

"It would help," Clint said.

"What if I was ta tell you when I saw them, they was wearin' Army uniforms?"

Neither Clint nor Molly had said anything in the saloon about Army uniforms.

"My friend," Clint said, putting his hands in his pocket, "I think we can do business."

The place where the dockworker had seen Collins and Tate was only two blocks away. An empty warehouse—not abandoned, but empty.

"Why would a perfectly good warehouse be empty on a busy waterfront like this?" Molly asked.

"Because somebody made damn sure it would be," Clint said.

"The Army?"

"Or Tate himself," Clint said. "What if he wasn't in the Army anymore, but the word didn't get around yet?"

"Wouldn't that kind of thing get around fast?"

"Okay," Clint said, "what if even the Army doesn't know it yet. He's out on his own, but hasn't actually resigned his commission yet. Maybe he just . . . walked away."

"And that's why your contacts, and even Jim West, didn't know about it yet."

"He kept his uniform, and convinced Jim to send for me."

"And Jim asked me to help you."

"And Tate asked me to help him, and none of us knew he wasn't in the Army anymore."

"So what's he doing, then?"

"Maybe," Clint said, "he's the one planning to assassinate the senator, and blame it on Dorence Atwater's delusion that Harlan Winston is Henry Wirz."

"And he has one man working with him?" she asked. "Collins?"

"And Collins may be the assassin."

"And this warehouse is his headquarters in San Francisco."

Clint put his hand on the door knob and said, "That's what we're going to find out."

# FORTY-SEVEN

The door opened. That surprised Clint. He thought they were going to end up walking around the building, looking for a window to use.

"Quietly," he said to Molly.

She reached for her gun.

"Leave it," he said. "Don't pull it unless you have to use it."

"How will I know when I have to use it?" she asked.

"Because I'll be using mine."

They entered the warehouse, closed the door behind them. There was a flash of daylight in the interior, but they couldn't help that.

Clint stopped just inside the door.

"What's wrong?" Molly whispered.

"We need time for our eyes to get used to the dark," he said. "The windows have been blacked out."

"I thought it was kind of dark in here, given that it's still light out."

He put his mouth to her ear.

"No more talking."

She nodded.

He could make out shapes in the interior of the warehouse, but couldn't see what they were. His instincts told him the building was empty. Tate and Collins were out. Maybe they weren't coming back.

He started forward, toward the shapes in the center of the large room. When he got there, he took a lucifer from his pocket and scraped it on his boot. It flared, startling Molly.

"Jesus!"

"Nobody's here," he said.

"How can you be sure?"

"I can feel it."

In the light from the match they could see two cots with blankets, a desk, some chairs. On top of the desk was a handgun and a rifle. He tried the drawers, had to light another match to see that they were empty.

"Look here," Molly said.

She had dug beneath the blankets on the cots and come up with two Army uniforms, one for a private, the other a colonel.

"I guess they've finally given up the Army," Clint said. "The gun and rifle are U.S. Army issue."

"Which doesn't mean they don't have some other weapons," she said.

"Right."

"So, if we telegraphed Washington, meaning it to get to Tate, we never would have gotten a reply, right?"

"Right."

"How would he explain that?"

"He'd say he was too busy."

"Would you have bought that?"

"No."

She dropped the uniforms back onto the cots.

"Now what?" she asked. "We've got a few days to find them before the senator arrives."

"First we have to get out of here."

She headed for the door they'd used to come in.

"No," he said, "we need another way out."

"Why?"

"Because that door was left unlocked."

"You think somebody's waiting outside for us?" she said.

"Maybe even our dockworker friend and some of his friends."

"We were set up?"

"I'm just being careful, Molly," he said. "Come on, let's find another way out."

They moved through the warehouse until they found a loading dock. Clint unlocked the door next to the dock and they went outside that way. He closed it behind them.

"Now what?"

"Well," he said, "we could go around front and see who's waiting for us, but that would tell Tate we're on to him."

"Doesn't the fact that we found the warehouse do that?" she asked.

"If there are some men waiting out front, the longer we let them wait, the more time we have without Tate knowing."

"What do you intend to do?"

"Talk to Atwater," Clint said, "see if he's working with Tate, or just being used by him."

"And then what?"

"I don't know," he said. "I'm making it up as I go along now."

# FORTY-EIGHT

Fester was bored.

He'd been standing in a doorway across the street from Atwater's paper—*The Reporter*—since morning, waiting for Clint Adams to put in an appearance. He was bored after one hour, so by now—several hours in—he was yawning and daydreaming.

When he spotted Clint, however, he came immediately to attention. The woman was with him, and they entered the building together.

Fester wasn't sure what to do. Wait for them to come? Run and tell Bellows now? That would take a while, because he wasn't sure where Bellows was. He wasn't in the habit of making decisions for himself, but he decided he would just wait for Adams and the girl to come back out, and then follow them.

He was quite pleased with himself for making this decision. Maybe he wasn't as stupid as Bellows was always telling him he was, after all.

\* \* \*

Atwater was not surprised to see Clint Adams approaching his desk, but decided to act as if he was.

"Well," he said, "what brings you back?"

"Did you think I'd give up on trying to save you from yourself, Dorence?" Clint asked. "If you kill Senator Winston, your life will be over."

"You don't think my life was over the moment they sent me to Andersonville?"

"You didn't have to let that ruin your life," Clint said.

"Maybe you didn't," Atwater said. "I didn't have much choice in the matter."

"Dorence—"

"If you're not going to help me, Clint, you have to stay out of my way."

"That's just it, Dorence," Clint said, sitting down. "I don't think you need help. I think you already have help."

"Really? From who?"

"That's what I want you to tell me," Clint said. "Do you know a newspaperman named Larry Gates?"

"I do."

"He was killed yesterday."

"That was actually in the newspapers this morning," Atwater said. "Why do I get the feeling you knew about it before that?"

"He was helping me with something, and somebody killed him. You wouldn't know anything about that, would you, Dorence?"

"No, I wouldn't."

"Do you have any photographs of Senator Winston here in your morgue?"

"Look around you, Clint," Atwater said. "This is not the *Chronicle*."

Clint took out the newspaper clipping he'd taken from Gates's hand and put it on the desk.

"This was in Gates's hand when we found him."

Atwater picked it up, looked at it, and then put it back down.

"It's not a good likeness."

"I know," Clint said. "I can't tell anything from it."

"Too bad," Atwater said. "If you got a look at the man, you'd agree with me, and help me."

"Again, about your help," Clint said. "Somebody has been shadowing us. You know anything about that?"

"Nothing."

"Have you seen Colonel Tate in San Francisco?"

"Who?"

"Fred Tate," Clint said. "He was a lieutenant when we were at Camp Sumter."

"I haven't seen Lieutenant Tate since we got out of Camp Sumter," Atwater said. "Why would he be here?"

"That's what I'm trying to find out," Clint said. "There are entirely too many people interested in Senator Winston's visit to San Francisco."

"Maybe Tate knows that Winston is Wirz, too," Atwater suggested.

Or maybe, Clint thought, he just wants Winston dead, for some reason. Since he didn't pay much attention to politics, Clint had no idea what Winston was involved in.

"I doubt it," Clint said, "but he's got something on his mind."

"So Tate is trying to kill Winston?" Atwater said. "I really don't care who kills him, as long as he ends up dead."

That wasn't what you usually heard from somebody who wanted vengeance, Clint thought. Usually in that case, the person wants to pull the trigger himself.

"Something's going on," Clint said, standing up, "and I think you know what it is. And I'm going to find out what it is. You can depend on that."

Molly, who never said a word the whole time, turned and followed Clint back up the hall and out of the building.

# FORTY-NINE

"You see him?" Molly asked.

"I do." Clint was impressed with how well Molly was able to check her backtrail. Each time they'd been followed, she'd spotted it.

"What are we going to do about it?" she asked.

"I think this time," Clint said, "we'll find out who he is and who he's working for."

"So we grab him?"

"I haven't decided," Clint said. "We can grab him or we can tail him. Let him lead us back to whoever he's working for."

"You don't think he's working for Atwater?"

"Don't know," Clint said. "He could have been watching Atwater. Or been waiting for us."

"If he was watching Atwater, would he leave him to follow us?"

"Depends on what his instructions are."

"And that brings us back to our question, doesn't it?" she asked.

"Grab him or follow him."

"Right."

He thought a moment, then said, "Okay, I say follow."

"Me, too," she said, and then added, "just in case I had a vote."

They lost their tail among the abandoned buildings in the neighborhood. The building housing *The Reporter* truly was one of the last of the occupied buildings in the area.

He was frustrated and confused, standing in one place but turning in circles, wondering which way to go. Once he figured out what to do, they would follow him.

If the man ever made a decision.

Fester was mad at himself.

He stood in one place, turning, trying to pick a direction. If he had to go to Bellows and admit he had lost Adams and the girl, that would just be admitting he was as stupid as Bellows always said he was.

Where the hell had they gone?

He stood still a moment, then admitted to himself that he had no choice.

He had to go to Bellows and admit that he had screwed up.

"Okay," Clint said, "he's moving. Let's follow."

"If he stops a cab, we're dead," she said.

"Haven't you noticed? There aren't many cabs around here. He'll go on foot for as long as he can. Hopefully, that'll be enough."

When Fester entered the saloon, he saw Edwards sitting with Bellows. Those two always seemed to be drinking when he was out doing the work.

"What the hell are you doin' here?" Bellows demanded. "You're supposed to be watching for Adams and the girl."

"They showed up," Fester said. "Went upstairs to see Atwater."

"And you figured you'd come here and tell us that?" Edwards demanded.

"No," Fester said, "I ain't that stupid."

"What did you do, Fester?" Bellows asked. "Just how stupid are you?"

"I followed them."

"And?"

Fester looked down.

"You lost them," Bellows said.

Fester nodded.

"Goddamnit!" Bellows said.

"I couldn't help it," Fester said. "It was like they lost me on purpose."

"On purpose?" Bellows said. "Oh, crap."

Clint and Molly stopped as the man went into the small, run-down saloon.

"Just getting a drink because he's frustrated?" Molly asked. "Or meeting somebody?"

"I'll go with meeting," Clint said. "Stand right here."

"I'll get out of sight."

"No," he said, "just stand here."

"But they might know me on sight—" she started to argue.

He smiled at her.

"I'm counting on that."

"Check the door," Bellows told Edwards.

The man got up and walked to the front door.

"She's out there," he said, "standing across the street."

"Shit!"

"What do we do?" Fester asked. "Go out and get her?"

"No, stupid," Bellows said. "She's the bait."

There were three other men in the place, and the bartender. They were watching Bellows, Edwards, and Fester simply because they had nothing better to do.

"They want us to come out there?" Edwards said.

"Right," Bellows said. "They followed Fester, but they don't know us."

"You guys ain't gonna leave me here, are ya?" Fester asked.

"We should," Bellows said, "but we ain't." He stood up. "Come on."

"Where we goin'?" Edwards asked.

"Out the back door," Bellows said. "Let them stand out there for hours if they want to."

He headed to the back of the room, then through a storeroom to the back door. Fester and Edwards followed.

When they got to the back door, Bellows opened it and rushed through it. He stopped short when Clint stuck his gun in the man's face.

"Where you going, boys?" he asked. "We haven't had a chance to talk, have we?"

# FIFTY

Clint forced Bellows, Edwards, and Fester back into the saloon. The other men came to their feet, unsure about what to do. The bartender froze. Clint figured the place was either always this empty, or it was empty because it was Sunday.

"I need some help," Clint said. "I need one of you to take the gentlemen's guns from them. I need another to go across the street and ask the lovely redhaired lady to come in."

Nobody moved.

"After that, you can all leave."

That galvanized everyone into action. One man left, went across the street to tell Molly to come in, and then kept going.

The other two took the guns from Bellows, Edwards, and Fester and laid them on the bar top.

"You two can go," Clint said.

They ran out the door, almost trampling Molly in the progress.

"Are you okay?" she asked Clint.

"Yes," Clint said. "Cover these gents, will you?"

She took out her Colt and said, "Gladly."

He walked to the bar.

"You know these men?" Clint asked.

"They come in here to drink," the man said, "but I don't know 'em."

"Okay," Clint said, "unload their guns and put them behind the bar, and then you can go."

"Are you gonna bust up my place?" the man asked.

"I don't have any intention of busting up your place," Clint said. "I only came here to talk to these men."

"If you don't mind," the bartender said, "I'll stay. It ain't much, but this place is all I have."

"Okay," Clint said. "unload the guns and stow them behind the bar."

"Yes, sir. Um, would you or the lady like a drink?" he asked.

"I'd love a beer," Molly said.

"Actually, so would I," Clint said.

"Comin' up," the man said.

"After you've finished with the guns."

"Right."

Clint turned to look at the three men, who were watching the gun in Molly's hand.

"She's the nervous type," Clint said. "She shoots people by accident sometimes."

"One time," Molly said, playing along, "I shot one person one time and everybody remembers it."

The three men exchanged glances.

"If I were you, I'd have a seat," Clint said. "Now."

They all sat down. The bartender put two beers on the bar. Molly walked over, picked hers up with her left hand while keeping her gun trained on the men.

"What's going on?" Bellows demanded.

"What's your name?" Clint asked.

"Bellows."

"And them?"

"Edwards and Fester."

The fact that Bellows answered for them pretty much meant that he was in charge.

"We followed Mr. Fester here from the offices of *The Reporter*," Clint said. "Dorence Atwater's office."

"Atwater?" Bellows said. "Don't know him."

"I think you do," Clint said. "Wait a minute."

"What is it?" Molly asked.

"This man looks familiar," Clint said. "Bellows, did you say?"

"That's right."

Clint pointed at him.

"You were in Andersonville."

Bellows looked as if he was going to deny it, then said, "That's right, I was. We all were."

Clint looked at Fester and Edwards.

"I don't know them," he said. "But I recognize you. You were one of the Raiders."

"I don't know what you're talkin' about."

"Sure you do," Clint said. "You were at the trial."

"Trial?"

"When we put a bunch of the Raiders on trial, you were there," Clint said. "But not on trial."

"I told you, I don't know anything about any Raiders," Bellows said.

"But you were at the trial," Clint said. "You remember the Raiders and the Regulators."

"Yes," Bellows said, "I remember them."

Clint looked at Edwards and Fester.

"Hey, we were just there," Edwards said. "We weren't with either side."

"So you knew Atwater at Andersonville," Clint said.

"No."

"How could you not?"

Bellows pointed and said, "You don't remember them. There were a lot of men in Andersonville."

Bellows was right about that.

# FIFTY-ONE

"Here's the way I figure it," Clint said. "Atwater's convinced that Senator Winston is Henry Wirz, so he convinces the three of you of that as well. Since anyone who was in Andersonville would like to kill Wirz, you all agreed to help him."

"Except for one thing," Bellows said.

"What's that?"

"Henry Wirz is dead. He was executed right after the war."

"If you really believe that," Clint said, "why are you helping Atwater?"

"I told you," Bellows said. "I don't know Atwater."

"Then why was Fester here waiting outside Atwater's office?"

"I don't know," Bellows said, "why don't you ask him?"

That was Bellows's first mistake. Fester was not smart enough to go along with that.

"Wha—" Fester said.

"He's confused," Clint said. "He needs you to tell him what to do and what to say." Clint knew that by how long it had taken Fester to make a decision earlier in the day. He had literally been walking in circles.

Fester looked at Bellows and said, "Ted, I don't know wha—"

"Shut up, Jake." Bellows sat back in his chair. "Okay, Adams, all you know is that we were all in Andersonville. We three know each other. And of course, we all know who Henry Wirz was."

"What about Lieutenant Tate?"

"What?"

"Tate," Clint said. "Remember him from Andersonville? He's now Colonel Tate. You're either working for him or for Atwater."

"Or with the colonel, or Atwater," Molly said.

"Good point," Clint said. "Are you working for one of them, or with one of them?"

"I'm not workin' with or for anybody," Bellows said. "These idiots, they work for me, but I have no idea why Fester was following you today. I suspect he might have recognized you from Andersonville—"

"Stop!" Clint said.

"That's it," Fester said.

Great, Clint thought. Bellows had outsmarted him and put the idea in Fester's head.

"Molly, take Fester into the storeroom," Clint said.

"Okay," she said, putting down her partially finished beer. "Let's go."

"Easy with that gun," Fester said as she walked him back.

Clint waited until Molly and Fester were gone.

"I'm willing to bet that among the three of you," Clint said, "Fester is the weak link. So I'm going to go back there and make him explain everything to me. Everything."

Bellows stared at him.

"He's bound to mess up somewhere," Clint said, "and then I'll get the whole story."

"Well," Bellows said, "in theory that sounds like a good plan."

"In theory?"

"Yes," Bellows said, "except for one little flaw."

"And what's that?" Clint asked.

Bellows leaned forward and said, "Even if there was a whole story to know, Jake Fester would not know it."

He sat back and folded his arms.

"Well," Clint said, afraid that the man was right again, "we'll have to see about that."

# FIFTY-TWO

Clint changed places with Molly and told her aloud, "Stay nervous."

"I'll shoot the first one who moves," she promised.

Clint moved into the back room, where Fester was sitting on a crate looking nervous.

"I don't know nothin'," he said immediately.

"Oh, come on, Fester," Clint said. "That's a lie. What's your first name? Jake?"

The man didn't answer.

"I'm going to call you Jake."

Fester shrugged.

"Listen, Jake," Clint said, "I understand you were at Camp Sumter; I understand you suffered. We have that in common. But I don't think you really want a part of killing a U.S. senator, do you?"

No answer.

"I mean, even if he was Henry Wirz at one time, he's a senator now."

"You were there!" Fester snapped. "How can you say that? If it's Wirz, he deserves to die."

"I agree," Clint said calmly. "If it was Wirz, he would deserve to die, but Wirz is already dead."

"Not according to—" Fester stopped.

"Not according to Dorence Atwater?" Clint asked. "Or did you hear it from someone else?"

Fester compressed his lips.

Clint moved closer to Fester and leaned over.

"I've been nice and calm so far, Fester," Clint said. "But you know my rep. I could stand back, draw, and shoot off an ear with no problem. Then another ear. Is killing the senator worth both your ears?"

Fester put one hand to an ear, then put it down quickly.

Clint looked around, spotted a supply cabinet, and walked over to it.

"Look at this," he said. "Candles."

He took out two white wax candles that were about six inches long.

"Here," he said. "Hold one of these in each hand."

Fester frowned, but did as he was told. Clint took out a lucifer and lit each wick. Fester was now holding two lighted candles.

"Hold them up," Clint said. "If I miss, I don't want to hit you."

"Wha—"

Clint drew and fired twice in quick succession.

"What the hell—" Bellows snapped at the sound of shots.

"Uh-uh," Molly said. "Don't move."

Bellows stared at the barrel of her gun, then sat back in his chair. Edwards looked as if he was going to piss his pants.

"Clint's just questioning him, that's all," she said. "Or shooting off some fingers. Maybe when he's done with him, he'll start on . . . you." She turned her gun to point at Edwards, who jumped, as if she'd pulled the trigger.

*   *   *

Fester closed his eyes as Clint fired, then opened them and looked at the candles. Clint had put out both flames without hitting the candles. Fester dropped both candles as if they were hot.

Clint reloaded and holstered his gun.

"Your ears are next, Jake," Clint said.

"Whataya wanna know?" Fester asked.

"What are we going to do with them for two days?" Molly asked.

They had all three men in the storeroom now, with their hands and feet tied.

"The police?" she asked.

"No," Clint said. "You're going to have to send a telegram to Washington. We need somebody to pick them up."

"What about until then?" she asked.

"If we give the bartender enough money, he'll close and hold them here until they're picked up."

"And who do we tell him will be picking them up?" she asked.

"We'll just say the government," Clint said.

"You can't do this," Bellows said. "You'll be lettin' Wirz get away."

"Fester said Atwater wants to kill him," Clint said. "Don't you believe in him?"

"You knew Atwater in Andersonville," Bellows said. "He ain't changed. He'll never be able to pull the trigger."

"You didn't kill Larry Gates, right?"

"I tol' you that," Bellows said.

After Fester had spilled the beans that they had all been contacted by Atwater, who recruited them to kill Henry Wirz, Bellows had opened up as well. Clint believed them. All they knew was that Atwater had recognized Senator Winston as Henry Wirz, and they wanted him dead.

"If you didn't kill Gates, then somebody else is out there gunning for the senator. So one way or another, he'll probably get killed."

"Unless you save him."

"That's right."

"But you won't," Bellows said.

"Why not?"

"Because when you see him, you'll know he's Henry Wirz," Bellows said.

"I doubt it."

"Well," Bellows said, "if he's not, then it's all been for nothin' anyway. You won't be able to charge us with anythin'."

"I don't care about charging you," Clint said. "I just want to keep you out of the way until Tuesday."

"Let us go," Bellows said, "and we'll stay out of the way."

"Good try," Clint said, "but I don't think so."

Molly gagged the three men, so they couldn't cry out, and then they went back into the saloon to make their deal with the bartender.

# FIFTY-THREE

What Clint and Molly did not know was that Atwater had been watching from a window as Jake Fester followed them away from the building. Atwater shook his head. Fester was terrible at it, and they were sure to see him.

Atwater knew he could not count on Bellows and his men now. Clint was sure to get Fester to take him to the others.

Atwater collected his jacket from the back of his chair and left the building. He had people to see.

Clint and Molly returned to the offices of *The Reporter* to find Atwater gone. No one knew where he had gone. There was a window near Atwater's desk. Clint walked to it and looked out.

"Look here," he said to Molly. "Clear view of the front of the building."

"So?"

"If he was looking out when Fester tried to follow us, he'd figure that we were going to see him."

"And grab him?"

"And make him take us to Bellows and Edwards."

"So he's got to figure he's on his own now."

"But is he?" Clint asked.

"You mean Tate and Collins?"

"My memory of Tate has always been as a smart man," Clint said. "If he's in town, as we suspect, maybe he's running Atwater."

"If the senator is not Henry Wirz, then Tate wants him dead for another reason."

Clint nodded.

"And I'm not knowledgeable enough of politics to know what his agenda is."

"But if Tate wants him so bad he's willing to give up his commission . . ."

"And he's not Wirz . . ."

They both stopped, because they didn't know where they were going.

"So what do we do?"

"We've been sending telegrams and nobody seems to be able to help us," Clint said. "Nobody knows anything about the senator."

"Or about Tate."

Clint shook his head.

"Let's check out Atwater's home," he said finally.

"You don't expect to find him there, do you?"

"No," he said. "If he figures we have his three men, then he's gone to ground."

"Or gone to find Tate."

Clint nodded.

When they got to Atwater's place, Clint forced the front door. The place was empty.

"Last time we were here, I didn't notice how messy this place was," she said.

The bed was a mess, bedclothes on the floor, some shirts and underwear there as well.

"Let's look around."

"For what?"

"For whatever we can find. I'll take this room, you take the other room and the kitchen."

She nodded, grateful that he was taking the messy bedroom.

Atwater entered the saloon down near the waterfront, the same one Clint and Molly had been asking questions in.

As he passed the bar, the bartender looked at him and nodded. Atwater went to a door in the back wall and entered.

"You're not supposed to come here," Colonel Frederick Tate said.

"I think Clint Adams has taken Bellows and his men out of the play," Atwater said.

Tate, dressed like a longshoreman, said, "That was to be expected."

"So what do we do now?" Atwater asked. "Where's Collins?"

"Collins is out doing his job," Tate said.

"Is he going to get rid of Adams?"

"If it becomes necessary to dispose of Clint Adams, I'll make that decision when the time comes," Tate said. "For now just stay away from him."

"How do I do that?"

"Easy. Don't go to work, and don't go home."

"Were do I go?"

"Anywhere," Tate said. "You know San Francisco better than I do. Do you have a woman?"

"No," Atwater said, "no woman."

"Well, find someplace. Go to ground somewhere until it's all over."

"How will I know when it's over?"

"You'll hear about it, believe me."

"What about Wirz?"

"Don't worry about Wirz," Tate said.

"I don't understand any of this," Atwater said, shaking his head.

"You were never meant to, Dorence," Tate said. "You were simply meant to be a good soldier—something you've been wanting since Andersonville, right?"

Atwater nodded.

"You weren't a good soldier then, but you are now," Tate said. "You only need be for a couple of more days."

"Yes, sir."

"Now go, and use the back door," Tate said.

Atwater walked past the seated man, moving to the back door.

"Are you sure you don't need me to—" he started.

"I've told you what I need from you, soldier," Tate said.

Atwater nodded and went out the back door.

# FIFTY-FOUR

Clint and Molly did a thorough search of Atwater's rooms. Clint came out of the bedroom as Molly was finishing up in the kitchen.

"Did you look at this little desk in the corner?" Clint asked.

"Yeah, I did."

Clint walked over to it. If Atwater did any of his work at home, it would be at that desk.

"You won't mind if I look, too?"

"Help yourself," she said. "Maybe you'll find something I missed, but don't expect me to go into that bedroom."

Clint laughed and opened the desk drawer. He sat down and stuck his hand into the desk, feeling around the sides and the back. He was rewarded when he felt a piece of paper at the back. He grabbed it and pulled it out as Molly came walking over.

"You found something?"

"Stuck to the back of the drawer, apparently," Clint said, taking it out.

"What is it?"

Clint held the slip of paper up so they could both see it.

"It's an address."

"On Drumm Street?" she asked. "Isn't that where we were?"

"Yup," Clint said. "This is the address of that dock-workers' saloon we went into."

"Are you sure?"

"Positive."

"So Atwater had a meeting there. What does that tell us?"

"He wrote it down so he wouldn't forget it," Clint said. "That means it was an important meeting."

"You think he met Bellows and his men there?" she asked. "Or are you thinking about Tate?"

"I'm thinking," he said, "that maybe we should go down there again."

"We weren't very welcome the last time," she reminded him.

"And we probably won't be very welcome this time ei-ther." Clint said. "That's not going to stop us from going."

# FIFTY-FIVE

They decided to go and get something to eat and discuss further what their next move should be. After walking a few blocks and not finding a likely place, they decided to go back to their hotel to eat in the dining room.

"Mr. Adams!" the clerk, Cal, called.

"Yeah?"

"This came for you while you were out," the clerk said, handing Clint a telegram.

"Thanks."

Cal gave Molly a long look, but she totally ignored him. She and Clint went into the dining room and got a table, which was easy because it was between mealtimes.

"Who's it from?" she asked.

He opened it and looked at the name at the bottom.

"Jim West."

"Why would he send it to you and not to me?" she wondered.

"You can ask him next time you see him."

Clint read the telegram.

"Well."

"He's back in Washington, and he's confirmed something for us."

"What?"

"Tate is not a colonel anymore," he said, handing her the telegram.

Molly read the telegram and put it down on the table.

"That's what it says, but it doesn't say why."

"I'm sure Jim wanted to keep the telegram short," Clint said. "And it really doesn't matter what the reason is. The fact is that Tate lied to me to get me here."

"Why?"

"He's either going to use me to pin the senator's assassination on Dorence Atwater," Clint said, "or he's planning on pinning it on me."

"So why don't you just leave town, like you said you might?" she asked.

"I'm not going to leave you alone," he said, "and I'm not going to let Tate get away with assassinating a United States senator."

"I'm touched."

The waiter came with their food.

"And I'm hungry," Clint said. "Let's eat."

By the time they had finished their food, Clint had decided to check out the address they'd found in Atwater's desk at night.

They were walking out into the lobby when Duke Farrell appeared.

"I've got somethin' you should know," he said to Clint.

"What is it?"

"Come back to the office."

Clint looked at Molly and they followed Farrell back to the office.

"I've been doin' some snooping," Farrell said, sitting behind his desk.

"And?"

"There's a guy in town," Farrell said, "he's known as *Poca Muerte*."

"Little Death?" Clint asked. "Why?"

"He's a killer," Farrell said. "For hire."

"Well, that explains '*Muerte*,'" Molly said. "What about '*Poca*'?"

"Well, apparently," Farrell said, "as deadly as he is, he's not a very big man. But he is dangerous."

"And you think he's in town because of Clint?" she asked.

"I think it's too much of a coincidence," Farrell said. He looked at Clint. "Do you think a hired killer being in San Francisco could have anything to do with why you're here?"

"Oh, yeah," Clint said.

"You think he could be here to kill the senator?" Farrell asked.

"Seems likely to me," Clint said. "You have any idea where he is?"

"That I can't tell you," Farrell said. "I've got eyes and ears out, but haven't been able to locate him."

"That's okay, Duke," Clint said. "I think we might have an idea about that."

"We are going to check it out tonight," Molly said.

"Think you'll need somebody to watch your back?" Farrell asked. "I mean, I can have a couple of good boys—"

"I appreciate it, Duke," Clint said, "but Molly's got my back and I've got hers. I think this *Poca Muerte* is going to be alone."

"Yeah, well, that's the word I get on him," Farrell said. "He works alone."

"Thanks for the information," Clint said. "It's helpful to know who we may be dealing with."

"If I get any more information, I'll let you know," Farrell said, then added, "both of you."

"Thanks," Clint said.

"We appreciate it," Molly said.

They left Farrell sitting behind his desk, shaking his head at their refusal of help from his boys.

"I appreciated that, Clint," Molly said.

"Well, you're my partner in this, Molly."

"We probably could've used some of the help he was offering us, though."

"Well, even if they were Duke's boys," Clint said, "I wouldn't have been able to trust them completely. I'm having a few trust issues lately."

"I can't blame you for that," she said, "not after Tate lied to you."

"Looks like it's going to be dark soon," Clint said. "Let's go outside and find a cab to take us down to Drumm Street."

"I thought we were going to wait until they were closed?" she said.

"After dark would be just as good," he said. "We'll go in the back. And maybe we can get the bartender to answer some questions."

"Are you sure about this?"

"I told you before, no," Clint said, "I'm just making it up . . ."

"As we go along," she said. "I know."

# FIFTY-SIX

By the time they'd reached the back of the dockworkers' saloon on Drumm Street, it was dark. Molly still wasn't convinced they were doing the right thing, though.

"I tell you what," he said. "Why don't you stay out here and keep watch. I'll go in and see what I can find."

"What if you walk in there and Tate and Collins are there?"

"That would mean we found them," Clint said.

"Wait a minute," she said. "*Poca Muerta?* Collins is not a big man, right? I mean, you'd almost say he was a small man."

"Or a little man," Clint said.

"So you've been thinking that since Duke told us about him?"

"I've been waiting for you to catch up."

"So wait," she said. "Tate's out of the Army and hiring a professional killer?"

"Looks like it."

"You know," she said, "I understand this whole thing less and less."

"Me, too," he said. "That's why I want to find Tate. So I can ask him what the hell he's been doing."

"Well, I'm going in with you, then," she said.

"Okay," Clint said. "Remember, no shooting until I start."

"Remember me?" she asked. "I start shooting when I get nervous."

"Well, not this time," he said. "Okay?"

"Sure."

He tried the back door and found it open.

"See," she said, "I haven't been in the Secret Service very long, but to me that's a bad sign."

He put his finger to his lips and opened the door. When she was sure he couldn't see her, she drew her gun and followed him in.

The inside was dark, and they could hear voices from inside the saloon. Clint motioned to Molly to close the door behind them.

After a moment their eyes adjusted and he could see the chairs, the cot. It looked like a smaller version of the warehouse.

"They've been sleeping here, too?" she whispered.

"Looks like."

He held up a finger to her to wait, then walked to the doorway that led to the saloon. There were three men there, including the bartender. Neither of the other two were Tate or Collins. For a saloon so close to the docks, it didn't seem to do much business.

"Only three men," Clint said.

"Should we brace them?" she asked.

"You watch the door," he said. "I want to look around a bit back here."

She nodded, moved to the door so she could see the three men.

He moved back into the storeroom and lit a match. By the light he searched the cots, looked underneath, but found nothing. Not even any extra clothes. Obviously, Tate and Collins—who may have been *Poca Muerte*—were moving around, never staying in one place for very long.

He moved to Molly and stood behind her.

"What should we do?" she asked.

"Let's wait for the customers to leave," he said. "Then we'll talk to the bartender."

"We could take them now."

"I know we could, but if they're just customers, I don't want to involve them."

"That didn't bother you in the last place," she said, "and we let them go."

"We don't need these two running out of here, attracting attention."

"What kind of attention?" she asked. "There's nobody around here."

"Let's just do this my way, Molly," he said. "Let's wait."

She shrugged.

"Okay, we wait."

# FIFTY-SEVEN

It took about an hour but finally the two customers left together.

"Okay," Clint said as the bartender turned the lock on the door.

He and Molly entered the saloon as the bartender turned away from the door. He froze when he saw them.

"What the—"

"Remember us?" Clint asked.

The man frowned, squinted, then said, "Yeah, yeah, I remember. Whataya want?"

"Just a few answers to a few questions," Clint said, "then we'll be out of your hair."

The barman—who stood at least six three and had huge forearms—folded his arms across his chest and cocked his head to one side.

"What questions?"

"Well," Clint said, "for one, where's the colonel? Or does he ever call himself that anymore? That's two questions, but feel free to answer just the first one."

"What colonel?"

"That was the wrong answer," Clint said. He looked at Molly. "Shoot him."

"What?" she asked.

"What?" the man said.

"Shoot . . . him," Clint said.

Molly looked him in the eyes and got it. She turned toward the bartender.

"Where?" she asked.

"Take your pick," he said. "In the knee, the elbow . . . the head."

Molly cocked the Paterson.

"Wait!" the man said, holding up both hands. "I don't know where the colonel is, I swear. He was here until last night. H-He's movin' around."

"Where do you know him from?" Clint asked.

"I served under him during the war."

"Were you in Andersonville?"

"No," the man said. "I, uh, missed that."

"But when he came to you for some help, you said yes," Clint said.

"Why not?" the man said. "All he wanted was a place to stay."

"So you gave him your back room."

"For a while."

"Did he come here when he left the warehouse?" Molly asked.

"Yeah."

"And you don't know where he went from here?" Clint asked.

"No."

"Okay," Clint said, "let's try something else."

"What?"

"The man who was with him."

"W-What man?"

Clint looked at Molly.

"Shoot him."

"Where?" she said again.

"Okay, okay, wait!" the bartender said, putting his hands out again. "You mean . . . Collins?"

"Is that his name, or the one he's going by?" Clint asked.

"It's the only name I know," the bartender said, "but it ain't his real name."

"I figured that," Clint said. "Have you heard the name '*Poca Muerte*'?"

The man wanted to say no, but he looked at Molly, who was still pointing her gun at him.

"Okay, yeah," he said, "that's the name Collins goes by."

"Did you know Collins in the war?"

"No," she said, "h-he was too young."

Clint figured that, but wanted to see if the man would lie.

"What's your name?"

"Ray Donnen."

"Well, Ray," Clint said, "I'm going to need you to make a couple of guesses about where you think the colonel might be."

"Look," Donnen said, "I don't know why he's here, or where he went. I can't even guess."

"Why not?"

"Because all I am is a saloon owner," the man said with a shrug. "That's all. He came in, asked if he could use the back room, stayed a few days, and left."

"You didn't know he was in town until he walked in your door?"

"Not a clue."

Clint looked at Molly, who shrugged.

"Look, I'm staying at the Farrell House. If you see him again, you send word to me. You may be loyal to the man, but he's going to commit murder and he has to be stopped."

"Murder?"

"That's right," Clint said. "I have to stop him, and I'd prefer to do it without having to kill him."

Donnen stared at him, then said, "Yeah, okay."

"Let's go," Clint said to Molly.

"That's it?" she asked.

"That's it."

They walked to the front door. As Clint put his hand on the doorknob, Donnen called out from behind.

"Hey."

"Yeah?"

"You serve with him?"

"Yeah," Clint said, "I did. I was in Andersonville with him."

"Oh."

"And I'm loyal to him, too, Ray," Clint said. "That's why I want to stop him, and keep him alive."

"Okay," Donnen said. "Okay."

Clint didn't know if that meant Donnen believed him or not. He and Molly went out the door.

At the last second Molly started to ask Clint, "Shouldn't we go out the back—" But she stopped short when somebody stuck the barrel of a gun in her ear.

# FIFTY-EIGHT

Collins took them to a rooming house. Clint didn't know what part of the city they were in. He was only interested in the gun that was pointed at Molly the whole time. He didn't know if the driver of the carriage was in on it, or was just being paid to drive.

When they reached the rooming house, Collins said, "Get out."

He had removed Clint's gun from his holster and stuck it in his own belt. Molly's Colt was stuck in the back of his belt.

When they were out of the carriage, it drove away. Collins did not exchange any words or cash with the driver.

"Inside," Collins said.

"Your real name isn't Collins, is it?" Clint asked.

"Like I told you back at the saloon, Adams," Collins said. "No talking."

"Right," Clint said, "I forgot."

He marched them up the stairs of a fairly new building that was being used as a rooming house.

"Inside," Collins said.

The door was not locked, so Clint opened it. He let Molly go first, then followed. Collins kept a good distance between them so Clint had no chance to try to bat the gun away. He was smart.

In the living room, ex-Colonel Tate was sitting on a sofa with one leg crossed over the other. He was wearing a plain black suit.

"Colonel," Clint said.

"By now you know I'm not a colonel anymore, Clint," Tate said.

"Oh, right. I'll just call you Fred, then. Or should we make it Mr. Tate?"

"I don't care what you call me as long as you tell me what the hell you think you're doing."

"How's that?"

Tate leaned forward, put both feet on the floor.

"You're spending time looking for me when you should be looking for Atwater. Stopping Atwater. That was your assignment."

Clint stared at the man, who seemed to be perfectly sincere. He turned his head and looked back at Collins. The gun was not in his hand anymore.

"Is this for real, Fred?" Clint asked. "You have Collins here bring us in at gunpoint to ask me that?"

"What's on your mind, Clint?"

"Well, for one thing, why didn't tell me you weren't in the military anymore?"

"Would you have taken this job if I had?"

"Job? A job is something you get paid for. This was more like a favor—that is, when I thought you were acting on behalf of the government."

"I never said that."

"You never said otherwise either."

Tate waved a hand.

"Semantics," he said. "The facts are the facts. Atwater is

planning to kill a United States senator because he thinks he's Henry Wirz."

"And who killed Larry Gates, Fred?" Clint asked. "Was it *Poca Muerte* here?"

"What?" Tate asked. "What did you call him?"

"Little Death," Molly said.

"What the hell is that?" Tate asked.

"Don't try to tell me you didn't know that Collins here is a paid killer called *Poca Muerte*," Clint said.

"What the hell are you blithering on about, man?"

Clint studied Tate. He hadn't seen him for years, and had only just become reacquainted. Still, he thought the man's confusion was real. Could it be that he did not know that his man was a hired killer? Who did he think he was?

"Collins—" Clint said, turning toward the man. The turn saved his life, and Molly's. He saw Collins's gun coming up, didn't know who his intended target was.

"Down!" he shouted. He tackled Molly and took her to the ground just as the shots rang out. As they hit the ground, he rolled until they were behind some furniture, but he didn't know if the armchairs were well stuffed enough to stop a bullet.

He waited for more shots, but they didn't come. How many had there been? Two? One?

"What happened?" Molly asked.

"Stay down."

He disentangled himself from her and got to his feet slowly. He looked around. Collins was gone. He walked over to Tate. He was still seated on the sofa, but there was a neat hole in his forehead.

"What happened?" Molly asked again.

"Tate's dead," Clint said. "Collins is gone."

"Why didn't he kill us, too?" she asked. "Why run?"

Clint looked around.

"I've got a better question," he said.

"What?"

He walked over to where Collins had been standing, looked down at the floor.

"Why did *Poca Muerte* leave our guns behind?"

# FIFTY-NINE

They got out of there fast, leaving Tate's body right where it was. They assumed the rest of the house was empty, but somebody would be coming in at some point, and would find Tate's body and call the police.

"We're leaving a lot of bodies behind," Molly said as they left the house.

"Can't be helped," Clint said.

They walked a good distance before they reached an area where they could get a cab. Clint told the driver to take them to the Farrell House Hotel.

They were in an enclosed carriage, so they assumed if they kept their voices down, the driver would not hear them.

"This blows part of my thinking right out of the water," Clint said.

"That Tate was behind the plan to kill the senator?" Molly asked.

"That's right."

"But then maybe he became a liability?"

"Tate looked genuinely puzzled when we started asking

about Collins as a hired assassin," Clint said. "I don't think he knew."

"Then who did he think Collins was?"

"I don't know," Clint said. "We'd have to check. Only I would've checked with Tate. He was my only Washington connection."

"What about West?"

"He's away from Washington more than he's there, but maybe he'd know something." Clint looked at Molly. "Okay, I haven't asked you this yet. Who's the head of the Secret Service now?"

"Henry Adcock."

"I never heard of him."

"I think he took over just before I came," she said.

"Can you telegraph him?"

"I guess," she said. "I've never really spoken to him myself."

"Who do you talk to to get your assignments?"

"My superior is Neil Summerville."

"Okay, telegraph him, then," Clint said. "Ask him about Tate, Collins, Winston, all of them." He wondered why she had never come up with these names before.

"I'm not supposed to contact them while I'm in the field."

"Break the rule," he said. "We need new information."

"Okay."

When they got to the hotel, he stepped down from the coach, then helped Molly get out and paid the driver.

"Has it occurred to you that maybe it's over?" she asked.

"How could it be over?"

"Tate's dead, we have the three men who were working for Atwater."

"There's still Atwater. And Collins."

"But Tate was the brains."

"Maybe, maybe not," Clint said. "I can't get the look on

his face out of my head when I asked about *Poca Muerte*. He had no idea what I was talking about."

"So maybe Tate wasn't in on it?"

"Maybe," Clint said, "but that doesn't explain Collins. He works for money. Somebody had to have hired him."

"All we have left is Atwater," she said.

"You send your telegrams in the morning," Clint said, "and I'll see if I can find Atwater."

"Tomorrow's Monday," she said. "We've got one day left before the senator gets here."

# SIXTY

Clint was not happy.

This whole thing had gone bad right from the beginning—like when he said yes. His instincts should have told him that something wasn't right with Tate, that Collins was definitely a wrong one, and that the whole Henry Wirz thing was some kind of a con. Only who was getting conned? And why?

In the morning Molly went out early to send her telegram. Clint agreed to meet her in the dining room for breakfast. He was seated there, drinking coffee, when Duke Farrell walked in.

"Mind if I sit?" he asked.

"I'm just waiting for Molly before I order. Have some coffee."

Farrell sat down and poured himself a cup.

"Got some news this morning, thought you'd want to hear."

"What's that?"

"Frederick Tate, ex-Colonel in the United States Army, was found dead last night," Farrell said.

"Where'd you hear that?"

"I have eyes and ears in the police department."

"Found dead, or killed?"

"Shot to death," Farrell said. "That the kind of thing you'd be interested in hearing about?"

"Very interested," Clint said. "I was there."

Farrell looked surprised that Clint would even admit that.

"Who shot him?"

"*Poca Muerte*."

Now Farrell was really surprised.

"You and the hired killer both walked out alive?" he asked.

"He got the drop on us, took us to see Tate, who I thought was his employer."

"Gunmen have been known to turn on their employers," Farrell pointed out.

"I know," Clint said, "but I thought Tate was behind this whole thing. Now I'm not so sure."

"'Not so sure' sounds mild for the way you feel."

"You're right," Clint said. "I'm completely thrown off by Tate's death."

"So Tate's death and the killing of Larry Gates are connected?"

"Very connected."

"And your senator is arriving tomorrow," Farrell said. "He'll be met at the train station by a large contingent, I hear. Your killer would have to kill him in broad daylight in front of a crowd."

"Well, since I never heard of him until you told me about him, you tell me. Is that something he could do?"

"Definitely," Farrell said.

Molly came in at that point. They both stood as she sat, and then Farrell excused himself and left.

"What did he have to say?"

"Tate's body has been found already," Clint said.

"Well, I sent my telegraph messages, one to each of them."

"We won't be able to depend on replies coming in time," Clint said. "We'll have to try to find Atwater today."

"And if we can't?"

"Then we'll have to be at the train station tomorrow when the senator arrives and try to make sure nobody kills him."

"And then you can get a good look at him and decide if he's Henry Wirz."

"Henry Wirz," Clint said, "is dead."

# SIXTY-ONE

They spent most of the day looking for Dorence Atwater. No one at Atwater's office had seen him since Clint and Molly were there last. They looked in a number of saloons in the area, but if he was drinking, he was doing it someplace else. They also checked his home, but there was no sign that he had been back.

As they left his home, Clint said, "I don't know where to look after this."

"What about the law?" Molly asked. "They'll be at the train station, won't they?"

"You tell me," Clint said. "The Secret Service should be there. Will they share the honors with the local police?"

"Probably not," she admitted.

"Well," Clint said, putting his hand on her arm to stop her. "Maybe we're wrong. Maybe the senator is not in any danger at all, now that Tate's dead."

"But you don't believe that."

He waited a moment, then said, "No. And I think the reason Collins—if that's his name—left our guns behind was to challenge us."

"Challenge us to stop him?"

He nodded.

"If he's challenging anyone, it's you, not me," she said. "With Tate dead, he's either been paid already or he's not going to get paid," she said. "Either way, he's really got no reason to kill the senator, except as a challenge to you."

"Well," Clint said, "whatever the reason, I think he'll be there tomorrow, and so will we."

As they entered the Farrell House, Cal waved at Clint from behind the desk.

"Message for you," he said, handing it over.

"A telegram?" Molly asked as they walked away from the desk.

"No, just a handwritten message from our bartender friend."

"Which one?"

She was right—they did have more than one. Clint looked at the name. It was the bartender who was holding Bellows, Fester, and Edwards for them.

"They got away," Clint said. "Bellows and his men."

"Oh great," she said. "Now we've got them running around again."

"They'll either leave town or go looking for Atwater," Clint said.

"And they may all be at the station tomorrow."

"Right."

"Maybe we should talk to the law."

"If we tell them that we're connected to not only Gates's death but Tate's, they'll hold us. We won't be at the station tomorrow."

"Yeah, but they will."

"And they don't know who they're looking for," Clint pointed out. "We do. Do you have anything on you to identify you as Secret Service?"

"No," she said. "Not when I'm undercover."

"Is there a chance somebody from the Secret Service will recognize you at the station?"

"I don't know," she said. "I've worked with Jim. Maybe he'll be there."

"If he was going to be there, he wouldn't have helped Tate get me here."

"Well, maybe one of my bosses."

"We'll have to wait and see tomorrow," Clint said. "It's all going to come down to tomorrow."

Atwater finally made his decision.

He hadn't used a gun for some time, but he had used one in the war, and he knew how to shoot. He'd read about Tate's death in the *Chronicle* that morning, and now figured it was all up to him. He was the only one who knew that Senator Winston was actually Henry Wirz. Although he hadn't really seen Winston in person, he knew he'd recognize Wirz when he saw him.

It was up to him now—avenge the dead of Andersonville, to avenge himself.

Collins was ready. His rifle was his best friend, and had never failed him over the years. Now it was going to help him get the best of the Gunsmith. He personally didn't care if Senator Winston lived or died, though he'd been paid to do a job, and he intended to get it done.

But the best part of this would be outsmarting and outdoing the Gunsmith.

# SIXTY-TWO

Clint didn't know how nervous he'd feel when that morning came. He knew there was little or no chance that Henry Wirz had been alive all these years. Even less chance that he had lived and become a United States senator.

But what if, when he saw Winston for the first time, he found himself looking into the face of Henry Wirz?

Clint knew that Senator Winston was arriving at the train station at 9 a.m. He and Molly came down to the hotel lobby at eight.

"You ready for this?" he asked as they left the hotel.

"I'm ready."

"I know the Secret Service always assume danger," Clint said, "but if you see any agents you know, you let them know it's more than an assumption this time."

"Right," she said. "I understand."

"And if you see Atwater or Collins, don't hesitate. Shoot."

"Got it."

They headed for the station.

*  *  *

Although the arrival of Senator Winston had been announced in the newspaper—and Clint still didn't know why the man was coming—the train station was not teeming with people. Either the denizens of San Francisco didn't read the paper, weren't politically active, or simply didn't care. Whatever the reason, Clint was happy he was not going to have to deal with shoulder-to-shoulder crowds.

Clint sent Molly in ahead of him. By the time he entered, she was on the other side of the station. Clint could pick out the Secret Service men scattered about. He knew that if he presented himself to them with his information—even if they recognized his name—it would be more of a distraction than anything else. The agent he approached would have to send for a superior, and they'd be talking to Clint instead of doing their jobs.

Clint stepped outside to look at the platform. Most of the waiting passengers were inside, but when the train started moving into the station, they would all go out to where he was standing.

Clint walked to the edge of the platform, but instead of glancing down the track, he looked up, to see where a shot might be taken from. There was the roof of the station, but it did not offer a clear view of much of the platform.

Clint walked the length of the platform, studying the faces of all the people, but did not spot Atwater or Collins.

However, somebody had spotted him.

As Clint was returning to the station, three men converged on him, and he knew he was about to be braced by the Secret Service.

Collins was going to use Atwater as a diversion. He knew the newspaperman would be there. He had to be. He would wait for Atwater to make his move, and that's when he would strike.

Under the noses of the Secret Service, and Clint Adams.

"Sir?" one of the Secret Servicemen said to him.

"Yes?"

The three men reached him, encircled him.

"Secret Service, sir," the man said. "I'm afraid I'm going to have to ask you for your name, and your gun."

"My name is Clint Adams," he said, "and I'm not giving you my gun."

The three men tensed.

"Sir, don't cause trouble."

"Believe me," Clint said, "I'm not here to cause trouble. Look, I'm here with a member of your service to stop an assassin."

"Sir?"

"Do any of you know Molly O'Henry?"

The three men exchanged a glance.

"A girl?" one of them said.

"You have female members," Clint said.

"Sir," the first man said, "please don't try to—"

"Do any of you know Jim West?"

That name gave them pause.

"Yes, sir, we do."

"Well, I'm a friend of his. In case you didn't hear me, my name is Clint Adams."

He looked at the three men. Their faces were blank, but then there was a flicker in the eyes of one, the spokesman.

"Clint Adams?"

"That's right."

"The Gunsmith?"

"That's right."

"Sir," the man said, "you can keep your gun, but I'm afraid I'll have to ask you to come with us."

"Are we going to talk to your boss?"

"Yes, sir."

"Then lead on," Clint said. "I want to distract you as little as possible."

# SIXTY-THREE

They took Clint to a small room off the main station. A man in his forties with slicked-back black hair looked up from a table, where Clint could see he had a map of the station and platform.

"What's going on?" the man asked. "You belong out there."

"This man looked suspicious, sir, so we asked him who he was."

"And?"

"He's the Gunsmith, sir."

The man stood up straight and studied Clint.

"All right," he said finally. "You stay, the rest of you back outside."

The spokesman stayed, the other two left.

"I assume you're the agent in charge?" Clint asked.

"That's right, Steve Ames. Do you have any identification on you, Mr. Adams? I mean, to prove you are who you say you are?"

"We're wasting time," Clint said. "No, I don't carry anything like that. If Jim West was here, he could vouch for me."

"West?"

"We're friends."

"I'd heard that," Ames said.

"I'm in San Francisco because Jim West asked me to come. It's a long story and we don't have time to go into it right now. There are two men in town planning to kill the senator."

"Is that right?"

"One is a man named Dorence Atwater, the other a man I know as Collins, but who goes by the name '*Poca Muerte.*'"

"Little Death," Ames said. "I've heard of him. He's a killer for hire."

"And he's been hired," Clint said.

"Adams, why didn't you present yourself to me when you got here?"

"For this very reason," Clint said. "I was afraid we'd end up in a small room wasting time rather than outside, getting into position to protect the senator."

"What do you know about the senator?"

"Nothing," Clint said. "I'm completely disinterested in him, except for the fact that I know there are two men who want to kill him."

Ames studied Clint for a few moments, then said, "Okay. What do they look like?" Clint described them. Ames looked at his agent. "Lockwood, get those descriptions to everyone."

"You have another agent in the station. Her name is Molly O'Henry."

Ames frowned.

"We don't have an agent named Molly O'Henry."

It was Clint's turn to frown.

"Are you sure? She's fairly new—"

"I know the names of every Secret Service agent, Mr. Adams," Ames said. "I'm in line to soon become assistant director. Believe me, we don't have a Molly O'Henry."

Clint stared at the man, then said, "Damn."

# SIXTY-FOUR

It was clear to Clint now.

Molly O'Henry's position had never been confirmed by anyone. Not by Jim West, not by ex-Colonel Tate. Clint had never even seen the telegram she supposedly received from Jim West.

He'd been duped, and he felt ridiculous for it.

Ames asked him to point out Molly. They went out to the station and she was nowhere in sight.

"So we have three potential assassins?" Ames asked. "One you brought here yourself?"

Clint couldn't find the words to explain how he felt about that, and Ames didn't give him the time.

"Never mind," Ames said. "You're here, and I'm going to put you to good use. If you see any of those three, you sound off and let my men know. But if it's you who isn't who you claim to be, God help you."

"Believe me," Clint said, "I wouldn't admit to being made a fool of if I didn't have to."

Ames gave him a hard look, and then walked away.

* * *

Clint couldn't figure out where Molly had gotten to. And he didn't understand what the point of sticking with him was when her ultimate goal was to kill the senator. He couldn't see what she had gained by attaching herself to him. It was general knowledge the senator was coming into San Francisco. She knew it, Tate knew it, Atwater knew it, and Collins knew it. With that many people wanting him dead, Clint figured the senator—whether or not he was Henry Wirz—was as good as dead.

He heard the train whistle.

Atwater heard the train whistle. It blew once. Then twice. And then again as it got closer. That was his signal to move. He touched the gun in his belt, then approached the door to the station and entered. Clint saw Atwater as soon as he entered the station. He had one hand down on his belt. Clint figured he had a gun there.

He looked around, saw that at least two Secret Servicemen had also spotted Atwater as a suspicious person.

The train whistled again as it pulled into the station.

"Gun!" one of the Secret Servicemen shouted.

Atwater heard the shout and panicked. He drew the gun from his belt as the train came into the station.

The Secret Service opened fire. Atwater was hit by so many bullets he danced in place for a few seconds before he crumpled to the floor.

All the Secret Servicemen in the station ran for the body and Clint knew immediately.

"It's a diversion!" he shouted. "A diversion."

They couldn't hear him as the train was screeching to a halt. Clint turned, saw Ames running, and stepped in front of him.

"What the—"

"It's a diversion!" Clint said. "We've got to go out on the platform."

Ames stared past Clint, then at Clint, at the look in his eyes.

"Okay, come on!" Ames said.

He and Clint ran outside as the train finally came to a halt.

"Which car? Which car?" Clint shouted.

"Come on," Ames said.

He followed Ames down the platform as people started to step off the train. At the end, the last passenger car, a small crowd had gathered, probably mostly newspapermen. Clint knew either Collins or Molly was in that crowd. Most likely Collins. He had probably been one of the men on the platform that Clint hadn't recognized.

"Get out of the way!" Ames shouted, pushing through the crowd.

Clint shoved through behind him. A couple of men came off the train and pushed people away from it as a third man appeared.

The senator.

Clint looked around frantically. Collins could have been any of these people, with a gun held down low until he needed it. The only thing Clint could do was get to the senator.

As the senator's Secret Service contingent was pushing people away, Clint ducked down low and rolled beneath the train, coming out the other side. Then he got on the train and rushed through, coming up behind the senator.

"Wha—" the man said as Clint grabbed him by the collar.

He pulled the senator back into the train and took his place. Now he could clearly see all the men crowded around the door, including Ames, who was still trying to fight his way through.

And there he was. Collins. Wearing a hat pulled low and a bulky coat. Clint had seen him on the platform and not recognized him.

"What's the meaning of thi—" the senator complained, coming out next to Clint.

"Senator—" Clint said, but Collins was raising his gun.

Clint drew and fired into the crowd. The bullet hit Collins in the left shoulder, but he had his gun in his right hand. Everybody on the platform hit the ground but Ames, two other Secret Servicemen who were out of position . . . and Collins.

Collins brought the gun up again. This time Ames and Clint fired at the same time. They both hit their target and Collins went down. Everybody else stayed on their bellies as the two out-of-position agents came rushing over.

"Stay alert!" Ames shouted, pointing at them. "There's one more somewhere."

Clint stepped down from the railroad car, gun still in his hand.

"Move!" he said to the others, all still lying on the platform. "Get away."

They moved, some of them getting up and running, others scrambling away on their bellies. Clint leaned over Collins, kicking his gun away.

"Dead?" Ames asked, coming up alongside him.

"Yes."

Ames looked up at the railroad car.

"Senator? Are you all right?"

"Yes, ah think so," Senator Winston said. "A-Ah believe that man saved mah life." The senator had a heavy Southern accent.

Clint took a deep breath, looked up from Collins's body, and took his first look at Senator Henry Winston.

He stared a good long time, just to make sure.

He'd never seen the man before in his life.

# SIXTY-FIVE

They brought both bodies into the small room Ames had been using, and closed the door. The senator was escorted to a cab and taken to a hotel, where he'd be safe.

Clint had gotten a good look at the man and was thoroughly convinced he was not Henry Wirz. That meant he had no further interest in the man. The only connection any of this had to Andersonville was Tate and Atwater, and the fact that Tate tried to use Clint.

"All I can think," Clint told Ames, "is that Tate planned to pin the senator's murder on me."

"But why?"

"I don't know," Clint said. "I don't know anything for sure, and with both Tate and Collins dead, I'll never know."

"What about the woman?"

"It makes me feel even more like a fool," Clint said, "but I think she probably is *Poca Muerte*."

"*Poca*," Ames said. "That's feminine, right? *Poco* would be a man?"

"That's what I mean by more of a fool," Clint said.

"Look," Ames said, "I'm going to ask you not to leave

town until I get a telegram from my boss, or from Jim West."

"Sure," Clint said, "sure. I'm at the Farrell House Hotel."

"Okay," Ames said. "I'll be in touch."

Clint nodded, started away.

"Hey!" Ames called.

"Yeah?"

"Thanks," Ames said. "Without your help, this might have turned out worse."

"That's nice of you," Clint said, "but without me, this might not have happened at all."

Clint was going to go back to the Farrell House, but he decided to first go to the Bucket of Blood on the Barbary Coast and pick up his saddlebags and rifle. As far as he was concerned, his part was done. The safety of the senator was up to others.

He went up the stairs and walked down the hall to Rooms 6 and 7. He still had both keys in his pocket. He thought he remembered leaving the gear in 6, so he went in there first. He was right the first time. He grabbed the saddlebag and rifle and left, going back down to the lobby.

The clerk was the same one who had been there when they left.

"Here are the keys to six and seven," Clint said. "I'll pay my bill now."

"You will?"

"Sure, why not?"

"Well . . . ain't the lady still up there in seven?"

"What?"

"I mean, you can pay for six, but if she's still using seven—"

Clint dropped his saddlebags and rifle on the desk and ran back up the stairs. When he got to the top, he moved more slowly down the hall. When he reached the door to Room 7, he listened, thought he heard movement inside.

"I know you're out there, Clint," Molly said.

"Molly?" he said. "Is that even your name?"

"It's as good a name as any," she called out.

"Come on out, Molly. It's all over. Atwater's dead, Collins is dead. The senator is safe. And the Secret Service knows about you."

"What about the senator?" she asked. "Is he Wirz?"

"Wirz is dead, Molly," Clint said. "I got a good long look at Winston. Wirz is dead."

"That's good," she yelled. "I'm glad."

"Come on out, Molly."

"What for?" she asked." Are you gonna take me in? For what?"

"Who killed Gates?" I asked.

"You saw Collins kill Tate," she said. "He must've killed Gates."

"And you haven't killed anybody?"

"Not this time," she said.

Clint remained quiet for a few moments, then asked the question he wanted to ask.

"Molly, are you *Poca Muerte*?"

Silence, then she said, "That's a stupid name, but it's as good as any, too."

"And were you hired to kill the senator?"

"Why does that matter now?" she asked. "It's all over. And it was all about politics, so it made no sense to me."

"Why'd you come back here?"

"I knew you'd come back for your gear," she said, "and I wanted to know. I wanted to know if Winston was Wirz. For your sake, I was hoping he wasn't."

"Why?"

"Because if he was Wirz," she said, "you would have killed him."

Clint wanted to protest, but found he couldn't, because he didn't know what would have happened if he'd looked up at Senator Winston and seen the face of Henry Wirz.

"Molly?"

No answer.

"Molly?"

He remembered that the room she was in had access from the window. He kicked the door open and rushed in, but it was empty, and the window was open.

He wondered if he'd seen the end of *Poca Muerte*, or Molly, or whoever she really was.

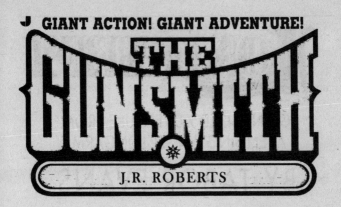

# GIANT ACTION! GIANT ADVENTURE!

## THE GUNSMITH

### J.R. ROBERTS

penguin.com/actionwesterns

M455AS0510

# LONGARM

## GIANT-SIZED ADVENTURE FROM
## AVENGING ANGEL LONGARM.

# BY TABOR EVANS

penguin.com/actionwesterns

M456AS0510